Some secrets don't stay buried

Prologue

They've all gone quiet. The others.

Jansen was the last to speak this morning. Just my name, like it hurt to say it. Then nothing. He hasn't moved in hours. Still sits on the starboard bench, back to me, coat soaked through. Head turned toward the water like he was waiting for it to speak.

He won't look away. I've tried. Shouted his name, shook him once. His skin was cold. Not stiff. Just… empty. I don't think he's dead. I don't think any of them are. But they've gone somewhere I can't follow.

Not yet.

The air doesn't move anymore. No gulls. No tide. Just that sound. Deep under the hull. A rhythm. Faint, but constant. Like breath beneath the water. We shouldn't have brought it up. It came tangled in the net just past the shelf. Heavy, smooth. I thought it was bone at first, maybe a whale's rib calcified by time. But it wasn't shaped like anything natural. It had carvings. Spirals. Marks that caught the light wrong. The captain said to bring it aboard, even when the crew hesitated. Said we'd found something old. Important.

We took it below deck. Lashed it to the mast post.

That night, it began humming. Just a little. A noise you couldn't hear but feel in your spine. Like your thoughts weren't fully yours anymore. We lost the first man two days later.

Sigurd went overboard during morning sweep. No splash. No cry. One moment he was there, coiling rope. The next, his boots were empty by the railing.

I thought he'd fallen. That was before we started seeing the ship.

It came out of the fog on the fourth day. Black sails, no flag. No sound of oars or crew. Just drifted past on a wind we didn't feel. I could see faces on the deck. Pale. Still. Not watching us. Not directly. More aware.

It passed without a word.

We should've turned back.

But the captain said it was an illusion. Weather tricks. Refused to speak of it again.

The humming got louder.

That was when the voices started.

Only at night. Only below deck. You'd hear someone whisper your name. Always your name. Right beside your ear. Then another voice, answering in a language none of us knew. Not shouting. Not mocking.

Just *talking*.

The kind of conversation meant to outlive its listeners. By the seventh day, we stopped sleeping. By the eighth, the sea went wrong.

It stopped moving.

Waves turned flat as glass. Nets came up empty, or full of bones too old to belong to anything alive. The water around the ship changed colour. Deep green, almost black, with veins of red like rust or something worse.

We tossed the object back overboard on the ninth day.

Nothing changed.

It returned the next morning. Same place. Same lash marks. Still wet. The captain tried to shoot it. The barrel exploded in his hand. He hasn't spoken since.

That was two days ago. Now they're all like him.

Mute.

Listening.

I hear footsteps above deck, but I know no one's walking. I see shadows that move without people. Reflections that don't match the light. And still, that shape in the fog. Closer each night. It doesn't drift anymore. It waits. We passed no islands. No light. No storms. But the map says we're weeks from shore, and we haven't moved in four days.

The compass spins.

The clock stopped at 2:17 a.m. and hasn't ticked since.

I tried to cut the ropes this morning. Thought maybe the ship was caught in a current. I looked over the railing.

There's no clean water.

Not really.

There's depth, yes, and cold. But it doesn't move like water. It looks back. Holds itself in place like it's waiting for something to enter. I dropped a line to measure depth. It came back up wet with salt and blood. I didn't try again.

Now I sit alone. Or at least I write like I'm alone. The others still breathe. But not like us. Not like men.

Jansen hasn't blinked in hours.

The humming's inside my chest now. I don't need to hear it to know it's there.

I feel it in my teeth. Not a sound exactly, more like pressure. Like the weight of a song you've never heard but somehow remember.

I'm not hungry. I'm not tired. I just wait. The body still breathes, still moves when asked, but the rhythm isn't mine anymore. It's slower. Measured. As if I've been calibrated to something else.

The stone is gone again. The others haven't seen it. Haven't looked. But I know. It's not where we left it. Not lashed to the mast. Not tucked in the crate below deck.

I don't think it's in the sea this time.

I think it's in me.

Not resting.

Not passive.

Turning.

Some nights, I feel it coil behind my ribs, a soft tightening, like lungs learning a new shape. I've stopped writing my own name. When I see it on old pages, it looks wrong. Not unfamiliar, just… **belonging to someone else.**

I think I've been carrying it longer than I knew.

Maybe it's not *inside* me.

Maybe it's *what's left of me.*

Arrival

The ferry moved slow through the fjord, cutting through water that looked more like glass than sea. Dr. Emil Strand stood out on the deck, one gloved hand tight on the railing, the other stuffed in his coat pocket where he kept the letter. The wind bit at the back of his neck, sharp and saltless, like the cold here didn't need the ocean to sting.

He watched the cliffs press in on either side, dark grey slabs rising straight from the water. No beaches. No gentle slopes. Just stone and silence. The kind of landscape that made you feel like an intruder, no matter how many years you'd studied the ocean.

He could see the village now, a scatter of buildings huddled along the waterline, roofs heavy with moss and snow. No roads in. Just a dock. A shop. A few houses sloped into the rock as if the land had tried to shake them off. Lysefjord wasn't the first place Emil had been sent for whale strandings, but it was the most remote. The agency's letter hadn't given much detail: three minke whales washed up in less than two weeks, each one found drifting belly-up or wedged in the fjord's narrow turns. Something about the pattern worried them. He didn't ask what. He was used to getting half a story.

The ferry horn gave a short, tired blast. A man on the dock raised one hand, more habit than greeting.

Emil pulled his duffel over one shoulder, tucked the letter deeper into his coat, and stepped off into the kind of cold that felt like it had history.

The dock creaked under his boots.

The man waiting looked to be in his sixties, lean-faced and wind-stained, with eyes set deep under a knitted cap.

"Strand?" the man asked.

"Dr. Emil Strand," he said, offering his hand.

The man ignored it. Just turned and started walking toward a parked utility sled with a flatbed and a sputtering diesel engine. Emil followed.

They rode in silence up the gravel track toward the village. The engine coughed now and then, but mostly it was the sound of tires over frost and the high whine of wind threading between buildings.

People watched as they passed. Not many, maybe a dozen faces in windows, a few in heavy coats standing outside the store, but none smiled. None waved. And none met his eyes.

It wasn't rudeness. Not exactly.

It was suspicion. Quiet and plain.

He knew the look. He'd gotten it in Alaska, in Newfoundland, on the Faroe coast. Small towns didn't like strangers, and they liked scientists even less. Scientists brought questions. Questions brought headlines.

And sometimes, those headlines didn't leave.

The utility sled skidded slightly as it turned toward a long shed near the water's edge. Two narrow doors swung open. Inside: the marine station. A single lab, a cramped bunkroom, and a tiny galley. Functional. Cold.

The driver cut the engine.

"Power's temperamental," he said without looking at Emil. "Diesel generator. Don't run the heater and kettle at the same time."

"Thanks," Emil said.

"Whale's down near the rocks. Still fresh. I'd get a look before the tide shifts again."

"I will."

The man still didn't move. Then: "They say it's not just the whales," the man said, eyes fixed on the water. "My brother saw it once. Said it had sails but no wind. Eyes but no crew. He stopped speaking three days later. Just whistled, like it was calling back."

Emil turned. "Who says?"

The man's eyes flicked toward the hills. "Don't stay too long, Dr. Strand." The man adjusted the rearview mirror, he wasn't checking traffic, there was none, but to look himself in the eye. Just once. Then he drove.

Then he left.

The door shut behind him.

Emil didn't unpack.

He left the duffel by the bed and grabbed his case, gloves, camera, sampling kit and headed back outside. The sun hadn't fully cleared the ridge, but the light was already going grey, bleeding fast into the late afternoon.

He walked down past the boathouse, toward the curve of rock where the first minke had reportedly lodged. The air was still. No gulls. No boat noise. Just the low lap of water against stone.

And then he saw it.

A pale shape in the water, caught half in and half out of the shallows, like something that had tried to crawl free and given up. Skin mottled grey and black, stomach bloated slightly, jaw slack.

But the eyes.

They were open.

Clouded. Glassy.

Staring not at the sky but back toward the village.

Like it had seen something before it died.

Emil crouched slowly, careful not to slip on the frost-crusted rock. He pulled on his gloves and scanned the body. No visible trauma. No propeller damage. No blood. Just… wrong.

He reached into his case for a scalpel, already forming his notes in his head: No signs of collision. No external haemorrhaging. Eyes remain open. Possible neurogenic cause.

Then he heard it.

Not loud. Not close.

But *exactly* behind him.

A voice. Low, male, rasped through something thick , like lungs full of seawater trying to speak. Not a shout. Not a whisper. Just… **spoken**, as if the speaker had been standing there for hours, waiting for the right moment to be heard.

"Dødningskipet."

He turned sharply, too fast, boots slipping slightly on the wet rock, one hand grabbing for balance. His chest tightened. Eyes scanned the treeline first, then the shoreline, then the path behind him. Nothing. No footprints. No shadow. No breath in the air but his own.

No one there.

Just wind, rough and sudden, curling around the ridgeline like it had changed direction mid-thought. Just water lapping dull against the stone. Just the ice shifting quietly behind him, slow and groaning, like something adjusting its weight.

He scanned the ridge again. Empty. Cold. Still.

Then looked back down at the whale.

Still dead.

Still watching.

That was the word he thought, not *facing*, not *turned toward*, *watching*. Not with malice. Not with intent. But with the stillness of something aware.

Emil didn't move. Not at first.

He stood there for a long time, breath fogging softly, hands clenched and forgotten at his sides, as if waiting for the voice to speak again or admit it had never spoken at all.

The voice had been clear. Real. He wasn't the kind to jump at sounds, not after years working on deck in bad weather, hours alone underwater with nothing but his breath and sonar pings.

But this… it wasn't imagined.

He scanned the ridge again. No movement. No figure in the trees. Just the same bare branches and rock-slick pine. He turned back to the whale and forced himself to finish the initial notes, though his hands were shaking a little now. Just from the cold, he told himself.

The tide had started to rise, slow but steady. He took a few swabs from the skin, scraped under the eye for tissue samples, then packed up. He needed to get the gear back in place before the power cut again. Already, the shadows were stretching. The fjord pulled darkness in early, too early.

Back in the marine station, the warmth was thin, barely holding at his back. He flicked the power on, waited for the fluorescent lights to sputter and hum. The computer groaned into life.

He pulled off his gloves, cracked his knuckles, and tapped in the first log.

Specimen 01:

- Species: *Balaenoptera acutorostrata* (Minke)
- Sex: Female
- Approx. weight: 5,800kg
- Condition: Moderate decomposition. Eyes open. No visible trauma.
  - Behaviour indicators: Unnatural positioning. Found facing shore.
  - Samples taken dermal tissue, optic, and baleen.

He stopped there. Finger hovering above the keys. He didn't type the voice. Not yet.

Later, while boiling water for coffee, mindful of the power warning from the driver, he heard it again.

Not words this time.

Just *music*.

Faint.

Somewhere between a moan and a song, drifting through the metal siding of the station. Emil stepped toward the window and leaned close.

The sound wasn't in the air. It wasn't in the wind.

It was coming from the water.

He walked down the short ramp to the dock. The surface of the fjord shimmered faintly in the moonlight, broken here and there by floating ice. No boats. No movement. But the sound was stronger now. Like a chant with no words. Not loud. But layered. Deep, slow tones rising and folding back on themselves, over and over, like a chorus sung by breath alone. It came from beneath the water, or maybe within the cliff walls, or maybe somewhere behind his own ears.

He stepped back. The wood underfoot groaned.

Then stopped.

The music was gone.

All at once.

Not faded , just ended. Cut off so completely it left an afterimage of silence behind it. Emil stood still, waiting for it to return, for any hint that it had simply shifted tones, moved higher or lower in frequency. But the stillness held. The kind that doesn't settle. The kind that waits.

He turned to leave the dock but paused again. The moonlight over the water was rippling slightly, but the wind hadn't changed. The air was still. Too still. The cold had thickened, not just in the air, but in his lungs, his fingertips, his bones.

A light flared just beyond the ridge. Faint. A flicker. Then gone. Not lightning. Not flame. It had moved in a straight line, slow, downward, like a torch falling underwater.

He blinked, but nothing moved.

Then, behind him, he heard a single breath.

Close.

Just one.

He spun, heart kicking hard, but saw only the path and the ice and the rock face beyond. No figure. No shape. Just the echo of that breath hanging in the air like fog that had forgotten to disperse.

He waited a beat longer, jaw tight, throat dry, then stepped back toward the treeline, boots crunching the thin frost that had spread while he stood there.

He didn't remember the cold coming in.

The next morning, Emil headed to the shop for supplies. Food mostly, batteries. The door creaked as he entered. Two older men leaned over a counter talking in Nynorsk, too fast for him to follow.

They went quiet the moment they saw him.

He nodded, gave a polite "God morgen," and grabbed what he needed.

As he stood at the till, the shopkeeper. Grey-bearded, eyes like flint, rang things up slowly. Then paused.

"You're the ocean man?"

"Marine biologist," Emil said. "From Bergen. Just here to investigate the strandings."

The old man slid the items into a paper bag. Didn't look up. "Don't stay long."

"Why?"

The man's hand hesitated over the receipt. "Sometimes things come up from the fjord that weren't meant to." He glanced at the back room, voice dropping a shade. "My daughter used to run this place," he muttered, more to himself than to Emil. "Before she heard the song." Emil said nothing.

Outside, the wind picked up. Dry snow scudded across the road.

The man spoke again, quieter. "This place… it listens. It holds what you say too loud."

Then he handed over the bag and turned away.

Emil stepped out into the cold, bag gripped in one hand, the door swinging shut behind him with a muted thump. Snow scraped sideways across the road in thin, restless threads, carried by a wind that hadn't been there a moment ago. The sky had dulled further, a flat grey pressing low against the rooftops and the village around him seemed to recede with each step, its shapes softening, as if being sketched backward into fog.

He adjusted his collar and started toward the station, the cold working its way beneath the layers, not sharp but deep, a kind of cold that settled into the lining of thought. The road was empty. No cars, no other walkers. Just old houses with their lights already out and windows that glinted too cleanly in the fading light, as if polished from the inside.

Somewhere beyond the far fence, a dog barked once, then went quiet.

He glanced down at the receipt still in his hand, half-crumpled, the ink already smudging from the damp. There were no prices. No item codes. Just the shop name, the date, and beneath it, handwritten in tight, careful script. A single word: **Holdfast.**

He stopped walking.

The word wasn't foreign to him. A maritime order, meant for storms. For survival. It meant *don't let go*. Not of the rope, not of the vessel, not of yourself.

The wind shifted again, sudden and low, curling around his legs like a thought unspoken.

He kept walking.

The research station came into view slowly, the windows dark, its antenna bent slightly from the last storm. He climbed the steps without looking back. Unlocked the door. Stepped inside.

The silence that greeted him wasn't empty.

It was *waiting*.

That night, Emil dreamed of the whale.

But in the dream, it was still alive, eyes wide, mouth open in slow, soundless panic. Its body pulsed, glowing faintly along the spiral of its back. And from its stomach, something pressed outward, like fingers, stretching the skin.

He woke just before dawn, drenched in sweat, the sheets pulled halfway down the bunk like he'd been twisting all night.

The generator had died sometime before.

No lights. No heat. Just dark.

And silence.

He got dressed fast. Hands numb. Breath visible.

His laptop battery was nearly dead, but the screen still glowed faintly when he flicked it open.

A new document was there.

He hadn't opened it.

He hadn't written it.

It read:

> *"The drowned remember."*
> *"They don't sleep. They just wait."*
> *"And now you've heard them."*

Deep Cut

He hadn't thought of the dive in years. Not because it wasn't worth remembering, but because some part of him had quietly decided not to. It had been a research assignment off the coast of somewhere he could no longer quite place, a sponsored survey, tied loosely to seismic drift studies, offshore turbine viability, or some other funding angle dressed in scientific urgency. The paperwork had blurred into other grants and contracts, the boat's name forgotten, the coastline nondescript. All Emil remembered, with any real clarity, was how the water had felt the moment he dropped beneath the surface. Not the chill of it, though it had been cold, but the weight. It had settled on him almost immediately, not the gradual compression of descent, but a heaviness that seemed to press against his bones the way darkness pushes against windows in an unlit room.

The first twenty meters had passed without issue. Routine observations. His instruments were all functioning properly. The tether line was taut, the array beacon still broadcasting its low, consistent ping from the benthic platform below. He moved efficiently, checking sediment levels and reattaching a power lead that had shaken loose from a sensor coil. The ocean was quiet, dull in its silence but not unsettling. At least not yet.

Somewhere around thirty meters, he felt something shift. Not in the water. Not even in the equipment. In himself. It wasn't vertigo exactly, nor a current. It was more like a tilt in perception, a moment where up and down recalibrated without asking his consent. The light dimmed, not gradually as it should have, but all at once, as if someone had flicked a switch above him. His dive light still worked, he remembers checking, but the darkness didn't respond the way it usually did. It didn't retreat. It absorbed. It sat around him like a thing with mass, thick and deliberate, like stepping into a place that had never wanted light to begin with.

He paused in his work, steadying his breath, double-checked his vitals. His tank pressure was normal. Heart rate elevated but not alarmingly so. No sign of narcosis or oxygen deprivation. No nitrogen bubbles rising too fast. Still, the feeling grew. The sense of presence, not of something seen but something felt. That was when he noticed the sound.

It wasn't loud. In fact, it didn't register as sound at first. It was more like a pressure, a low-frequency tone that sat in the jaw, in the teeth, behind the eyes. At first he assumed it was equipment interference. A signal bleed, a motor resonance from the ship above. But it didn't pulse like machinery. It was sustained. Constant. Tonal in a way that defied categorization. The kind of sound that feels less heard than remembered, the kind of sound that reaches backward.

He turned slowly, scanning the seafloor beneath him. The sediment had shifted. He hadn't touched it, hadn't been close enough to disturb it, and there was no current strong enough at that depth to have caused the pattern he saw forming: a gentle, slow swirl, wide and shallow like the beginning of a vortex, a spiral not drawn but implied. He blinked. It was gone.

He checked his depth gauge again. Thirty-six meters. He hadn't descended, but he hadn't stayed still either. His arms felt heavier now, legs looser, as if the pressure wasn't just surrounding him, but settling in. Something brushed his awareness then. Not a sound or image, but a presence that registered with absolute clarity. It wasn't a hallucination. It wasn't imagination. He didn't *see* anything, not exactly. But he knew, with the kind of certainty you don't question in the moment, that something below him had taken notice.

Not as prey. Not as intruder.

As participant.

That was when the blackout hit. Three seconds, no more. He remembered the count as if it had been stamped into his memory: one, two, three, then the sudden lurch of consciousness returning, lungs tight, arms drifting. When he reoriented himself, he was three meters deeper. No damage to his suit. No change in his vitals. But something in his mind felt scratched.

He should have surfaced. That would have been the professional response, the correct protocol. He was alone, after all, and the risk matrix didn't favour solo continuation after unexplained loss of consciousness. But instead, he hovered there for just a moment longer, suspended between pressure and paralysis, between instinct and curiosity. There had been a shape then, maybe just a trick of the light, maybe just a figment born of pressure and silence. It was low and long and seemed to blend with the seafloor until it didn't. He couldn't describe it then, and he couldn't now, only that it had been there in the way some things are present just beyond the edge of knowing.

Eventually, he'd kicked upward, breath slow, ascent measured. The ship greeted him as expected. The crew hadn't noticed the blackout. His readings had recorded nothing unusual. But something had changed. Not in the ocean. Not on the ship. In him.

And then he'd buried the dive, filed it away, skipped the full report, moved on to the next research site. It was easy to do. No one had died. No footage had corrupted. No data anomalies to justify further analysis. Just a gap. A memory held too loosely. A dive he could forget.

Until now.

Now, standing in the marine station's lab, staring at blood that didn't clot and tissue that didn't die, he realised something with a kind of quiet dread: He had heard the spiral before. He had just refused to listen.

He hadn't opened the old dive log in years. The worn black cover still bore his name in faded silver ink, half-peeled by salt and time, the corners frayed from years of dry storage and occasional displacement.

He kept it with his other notebooks. Those packed crates of half-recalled expeditions, field tags, bent tide charts, and waterproof pencils whose tips had long since gone soft. He'd kept telling himself he'd throw it out eventually. He never did.

It took him longer than it should have to find the right section. The dive wasn't even properly labelled. Just a half-page entry between two larger notes about sediment ratios and drift lines near the Faroe shelf. When he saw the entry, the first thing that struck him wasn't the content but the handwriting. It was undeniably his, sharp slanted print, always slightly downhill on the right margin. But the words felt foreign, like reading someone else's account written in a language just close enough to fool the eye.

Dive #12 - second shift

Standard descent. 35m depth. Full power across comm and light rig.
Instrument relay holding.
Minor spatial disorientation noted. Blackout confirmed via timer
(approx. 2–3 sec). No known trigger.
No evidence of physiological event. Returned to vessel. No damage
logged.

He ran his thumb over the indentation of the ink, as if touch might conjure more than memory. The tone was clinical, nearly sterile. The kind of report a cautious scientist writes not out of truth but out of expectation. Curated, diluted, made presentable for scrutiny. Nothing in it reflected the weight he'd carried since. Nothing about the darkness. Nothing about the presence. Nothing about how he'd felt watched not just during the dive, but afterward, in the cramped berth where the lights flickered once before sleep, where water beaded on the porthole in symmetrical spirals that seemed to fade before he could call anyone else to look.

What unsettled him most, though, wasn't the omission.

It was the drawing.

Tucked in the corner of the page, almost beneath the margin line. It was a faint, looping shape done in pencil. He hadn't seen it before. He would've remembered it. Would've marked it, asked himself what it meant. But there it was, sketched in thin graphite, no label, no context. A single spiral, done with a steady hand. Three turns inward. Evenly spaced. Precisely etched. Nothing random about it.

He stared at it for a long time. There was no tremble in the lines, no pause marks, no corrections. Whoever drew it had done so deliberately and had done it once. He turned the page, then back again. The spiral remained, faint but sure. His mouth felt dry, but he hadn't stopped breathing. He just hadn't noticed the breath.

He closed the log and stood up, paced the room once, and then went to his laptop. The blood samples were still logged from the earlier whale dissection, and he began running back through the data, looking for something, anything, that would justify the rising knot behind his ribs.

Instead, he found nothing new. The cells still weren't degrading. The saline control had already clouded, the tissue should've softened, but it remained whole. More than that, it had begun clustering. That hadn't happened earlier. Under the microscope, he saw a soft massing near one edge of the slide, a folding in of structure, not decay but aggregation.

He blinked and adjusted the focus, noting a pattern emerging in the tissue. Not just directionality. Not just movement.

Formation.

Something was taking shape in the corner of the slide.

He leaned in.

The spiral wasn't perfect, not geometric, not drawn.

But it was familiar.

Each time he saw it, on the stone, in the journal, under the lens, it wasn't new. It felt like the same spiral, just closer. Like it had been approaching him all along, turn by turn.

He snapped off the light and stepped back from the desk. The memory of the dive log still throbbed in the front of his mind. The blackout. The shift. The missing seconds. And now the drawing. It wasn't a copy of what he saw under the microscope. But it was close. Too close to ignore.

He returned to the notebook, flipped back to the page with the entry, and studied it again. The spiral looked older now, somehow more permanent. His own memory seemed to have caught up to it, as if it had always been there, and he had simply failed to notice.

But that wasn't what scared him.

What scared him was the thought that maybe it hadn't always been there.

Maybe it had *appeared*.

Inserted itself back into the record.

Or worse: maybe *he* had inserted it. Not now, not today, but *then*, in the hours after surfacing, when he still felt like something inside him hadn't fully come up with the rest of his body.

Maybe he had drawn it without knowing why.

Maybe he had remembered it before he knew it was something worth forgetting.

And if that were true, if the spiral had touched him once before, then he had never really left it behind.

He wasn't returning. He was arriving. The centre wasn't ahead. It had always been behind his eyes.

Emil sat with the notebook on the edge of the stainless-steel lab bench, his elbows pressed against his knees, fingertips curled tight beneath his thighs. The room around him buzzed with the low, mechanical breath of the facility: the hum of refrigeration units, the dry click of the overhead light relay, the faint wheeze of the heating pipe in the corner. It was familiar noise, sterile and predictable, and yet none of it could mask the feeling that something inside the space was listening, something that existed between the sounds, suspended in the quiet moments when machines took a breath.

The logbook was still open, the spiral visible like a mark left behind by a thought he hadn't meant to have. It wasn't just strange, it was wrong in its comfort, in how his eyes kept returning to it like the mind returning to a word half-forgotten. The longer he looked at it, the more certain he became that it hadn't been there when he first flipped the page. And yet now, the graphite looked smudged, faint at the edges, like it had been there for years. Not just aging in the physical sense but remembered by the page itself.

He tried to shake the thought. He picked up the notebook, checked the neighbouring entries. No other drawings. No other spirals. Just data: temperatures, pressure readings, sediment ratios. Facts and figures. Objective records of observable phenomena. But the page with the spiral didn't behave like the others. It resisted being dismissed. It demanded return.

He flipped back to it again.

The spiral had shifted.

Not a lot. Just a little. The centre turn, which he could've sworn was tightly wound just an hour ago, now seemed slightly more open, like it had relaxed, like it had... exhaled. He checked the edge of the page for warping. None. Held it under the lamp. No tricks of light or shadow.

The drawing had changed.

No part of his mind wanted to believe that. No rational framework allowed for it. He set the notebook down, hard enough to slap the desk, as if force might return reality to a more familiar setting. He stood, paced the room once, twice, opened the freezer door and let the sterile cold hit his face. The whale samples were there, exactly as he'd left them. Labelled. Sealed. Unmoving.

But the air felt thicker than it had earlier. Not colder, *denser*. Like the lab was full of water he hadn't noticed rising.

He sat again, pulled the notebook back toward him, and opened it without hesitation this time. The spiral still sat on the page, now joined by a second, smaller one in the upper right corner. It hadn't been there before. That much he was certain of.

This one was sloppier. The graphite lighter, the edges hesitant. Like a child's attempt to mimic an adult's drawing. Or like a hand trying to recreate a symbol without understanding why. He stared at it until his eyes watered, until the pencil lines blurred into motion and he had to blink hard to clear them.

He flipped back to the inside cover, where he sometimes scribbled notes in the margin: dates, meal rations, dive shifts, location codes. At the top corner, written in his hand but not in any ink he remembered using, were the words:

CENTRE ISN'T WHERE YOU STOP IT'S WHERE YOU WAKE UP He didn't remember writing it. He didn't remember thinking it. But it was his voice in the phrasing, simple, precise, stripped of metaphor. The kind of thing he'd say to himself when trying to distil a problem to its core. Except this wasn't a reminder. It was a warning.

He closed the book.

Then opened it again.

The second spiral was gone.

He stood very still, the kind of stillness that doesn't come from calm but from pressure, internal, invisible, the body holding itself like a glass full to the brim. His eyes burned, not from fatigue, but from refusal. The notebook sat in front of him, perfectly mundane. Perfectly silent. And yet its pages felt warm. Not to the touch, but in a way that suggested *use*, as if they'd been handled, turned, remembered by someone else before being handed back to him.

A small sound broke the silence, soft, mechanical. The printer in the corner of the lab, dormant for days, clicked once and began to whir. Emil turned slowly, half expecting nothing to be there, half certain something would be.

A single sheet of paper emerged.

He approached it cautiously, like it might vanish if startled.

The page was blank except for a symbol in the centre, printed in high-resolution ink, exact and mathematical.

A spiral.

But not his. Not the one from the notebook. This one had no central endpoint. It turned inward forever.

Beneath the image, typed in black, sans-serif font:

You are remembered.

Emil did not move.

The paper was still warm in his hands.

Frozen Water

The bone cracked, not clean, but dull, like wood too soaked to split.

Emil exhaled through clenched teeth. The blade had stalled halfway through the rib. The skin had come easy. Bloated and thinned, but the bone was dense, unnaturally cold, like it had never felt air.

Overhead, the lights flickered again. Pop. Buzz. Pause. The lab's hum fell into silence for half a second too long. He didn't trust the generator to last the day.

The whale steamed in the tarp, briny and sharp, but under the rot, there was something else. Not decay. Memory.

He pushed the saw again. It gave with a sound like wet stone grinding loose. The sound it made was thick and dull, not the clean snap he expected.

He stepped back, exhaled, and carefully widened the cut.

No blood.

No smear, no clot, not even a drying rim. The cavity was too clean. The organs sat pale and slack, as if emptied of purpose. The heart had folded in on itself, not collapsed, just… surrendered. No rupture. No wound. No effort to survive. Just... *emptiness*.

He peeled back the stomach lining. Inside, nothing.

No krill. No plastic. No debris.

Except. wait.

Then. There. A dull shape, tucked deep in the stomach fold. No tissue wrapped it. No bile. Just waiting.

He pulled it out. A stone. Same spiral. Same fracture.

He stared at it for a full minute before realising he'd stopped breathing. It wasn't just that the stone was identical, it was cleaner. The edges sharper, the fracture line more defined, like it had healed into a more deliberate shape.

Emil set it down, gently, as if afraid it might shatter or respond.

He backed away from the table without meaning to, bumping into the metal cart behind him, the clang too loud in the stillness.

His gloves felt too tight. The room, too small. And somewhere in the back of his mind, the thought came unbidden: *What if the stone hadn't come from the whale? What if the whale came for the stone?*

Impossible. He stepped back without meaning to. The table groaned.

"Not again," he whispered. But the air didn't answer. It listened.

Lines. Spirals. A single gouged rune cut deep through the centre, right through a natural fracture that had healed smooth over time.

His stomach tightened. It looked exactly like the photograph he'd received in Oslo. Not just similar, *identical*. The same fracture line through the spiral's outer arc. The same wear along one edge, as if a thumb had rested there, again and again, over centuries.

Exactly like the stone the woman from Scotland had mentioned, the one she claimed surfaced and vanished three times across two coasts and four decades.

He turned it over, it was warm in his palm. The warmth came from within, low, steady, the temperature of breath in a closed room.

He stared at it for a long time, unsure whether it was minutes or just long enough to lose track of everything else. The markings weren't random. The spiral wasn't decorative. It felt... recursive. Purposeful. Not art. Not even warning. More like *instruction*.

It didn't pulse, exactly, but it held a kind of pressure. As if it were *aware* of being touched. As if something inside it had noticed *him*.

He placed it in a sample bag, double-sealed it, labelled it with steady hands: **"Foreign Object A."**

He almost wrote "alive." But didn't.

By mid-afternoon, the sky had hollowed out. Not overcast or shadowed. Just... gone.

The wind had vanished. The fjord looked like poured iron.

Emil moved fast now, not from urgency, from instinct. He scraped tissue, tagged samples, snapped photos with hands that shook more than the cold could explain.

Every action felt rote, like science done in a dream. He tried narrating his notes aloud, but the words came out flat. Mechanical.

"Liver... pale. Fibrous collapse. Lung tissue..." He stopped.

The sound of his own voice, clinical and deliberate just moments before, now rang out through the lab like a trespass, each syllable sharp-edged and unnatural against the sudden stillness pressing in from the walls. It wasn't just loud. It was wrong, dissonant somehow, as if the air inside the room had forgotten how to carry human sound.

He stopped mid-sentence, mouth still open, then slowly turned toward the window without even realizing he'd done it.

Beyond the glass, the fjord stretched wide and motionless, not in calm, but in something deeper, something more deliberate. The water, once living with the soft rhythm of tide and current, now resembled a sheet of slate, colourless and inert, as if it had settled into a state beyond reflection. There were no ripples. No wind trails. No hint of life in the trees above the cliffs. The gulls, so common even in winter, were gone. Not hidden. Gone.

And still, the sensation was not one of absence, but of focus.

The fjord wasn't still.

It was watching.

Not metaphorically, not as a figure of speech or a projection of Emil's fatigue, it was the unmistakable sense of being observed, of something vast and indifferent fixing its attention not on the building, or the station, or the lab, but on him specifically, as if his presence had somehow triggered an awareness buried beneath the surface of water that no longer behaved like water at all.

He couldn't explain the sensation in scientific terms. Not yet, but it settled behind his eyes and along his spine like a weight, not oppressive, but precise. Measured.

And then the lights went out.

The lab lights died at 5:03.

One pop. One flicker. Then silence so total it made the room feel smaller. Emil didn't move at first. He waited to hear the generator catch, but it didn't.

The silence held. Too still.

He crossed to the breaker with his headlamp on. The switches flipped, but nothing caught.

Back at the tray, the stone waited. It hadn't moved. But it had changed. Frost spidered across the plastic like veins, looping outward in perfect arcs. It wasn't spreading.

Growing.

He leaned close. The spiral beneath the frost had thickened. As if redrawn. Recut.. Without the hum of the heaters, the building felt *empty* in a way it hadn't before. Too open. Too quiet.

He grabbed his headlamp from the shelf, clipped it on, and moved to the breaker panel. Flipped the switches one by one.

Nothing.

Back in the lab, the bagged stone sat exactly where he'd left it, centred on the metal tray like it had been placed for viewing. But something had changed.

It had frosted over.

Not fogged. F**rosted**.

Thin white ice crystals curled across the inside of the sample bag, forming delicate structures that shouldn't have existed without moisture. They spread outward in slow arcs, each curve measured and branching, not like random cold, but like growth.

Like fingers. Like filaments. Like memory trying to root itself.

He moved closer. The air in the lab had dropped by ten degrees at least. Probably more. His breath fogged thick and fast now, every exhale a cloud of urgency. He reached for the wall gauge.

Dead.

No reading. Just a blank screen. The backup battery light blinked once, then went out.

He turned back toward the tray. The frost had spread. It was blooming now, pushing outward in a spiral, feathering in slow motion across the plastic.

He reached out. Stopping himself. A sound had entered the room. Not loud. Not directional. But there.

Low, sustained, like something humming from the corner of the floor. Or the base of his skull. Not sound exactly. More like a tone his body knew how to interpret, even if his ears didn't.

It vibrated faintly in his molars. He stepped back.

It stopped.

Instant. Precise.

He stood still for several long seconds, listening, watching, breathing fog into the silence. He didn't touch the bag again.

He didn't sleep that night. Not really. He lay in the bunk with the lamp still on, fully dressed, boots laced so tight they pinched. His coat was open, but he hadn't taken it off.

He listened.

The wind came up around midnight. A dry rustle clawing at the siding, slipping into seams, whispering against the vents. Not gusts. Not storm wind. Just *movement.*

Every few minutes, it stopped.

Like it was waiting for him to move.

Then footsteps.

Soft. Slow. On the gravel outside.

He sat up, heart hammering. The wind didn't stop, but the footsteps paused. Then came again.

Then a tap at the window.

There was a sound, just one. A single knock, sharp and deliberate, like the rapping of a knuckle on glass. It wasn't a scrape, and it wasn't accidental. It landed with the kind of intention that made the skin along his arms tighten, as if the room itself had been addressed.

Emil turned toward the window, heart already picking up speed, gaze sweeping the room for a shape that wasn't there. Nothing moved. The air felt flatter than before, and even the soft whir of the equipment behind him seemed to fall back, as if the machines were hesitating to intervene.

Then the sound came again. A second knock. Identical in tone and placement.

He rose from the chair, moving slowly, not out of fear exactly, but out of caution, the kind that comes when something feels just a little too exact. With each step toward the glass, the sense of being observed pressed tighter, as if he were walking not toward a window, but toward something watching through it.

He reached out and turned off the lamp. The room dropped into low contrast, lit only by the pale, washed-out glow of the moon spilling across the fjord. Outside, the landscape held its breath, silver light glinting across frozen ground, the water still, the dock empty, the trees at the ridge unmoving.

A boy stood by the dock one morning, drawing circles in the frost with a stick. He looked up at Emil as he passed and whispered: "They never blink." Then he went back to tracing, as if the words had never left his mouth.

No figures. No shadows. No signs of disturbance. Not even footprints across the frost that had formed since dusk.

He leaned toward the glass, hand hovering close but not touching. His own face stared back at him, drawn and exhausted, features hollowed by too many sleepless nights. It was the same reflection he'd seen every day for the past week, except this time, something about it didn't feel quite right.

Then the reflection blinked.

He hadn't.

He was sure of it, absolutely, without question. He had remained still, unblinking, holding his breath. But the man in the glass had moved. The lids had dropped slowly and reopened with a slight shift in expression, something barely perceptible but unmistakably different.

His own face was looking back at him, yes, but there was something else in it now. Not recognition. Not mimicry. Something closer to *anticipation*.

He stepped back from the window carefully, one foot behind the other, never taking his eyes off the glass. He moved not like someone startled, but like someone trying to leave a room without waking the thing inside it.

His breath stayed tight in his chest, ears filled with his own pulse. The reflection hadn't done anything else, no smile, no tilt of the head. Just that one, slight delay. Enough to unhook something in his brain.

He sat on the edge of the bunk, light still off, trying to slow his breathing. Wind scraped across the siding like fingers. He rubbed his temples hard, trying to clear whatever fog had crept in behind his eyes.

Stress. Lack of sleep. Residual adrenaline. That's all it was.

It had to be.

He switched the lamp back on. Nothing in the window but his own pale face, mirrored now in proper sync.

Still, he didn't lie down. Just sat.

Staring.

Listening.

The tapping didn't return that night.

But the quiet was worse.

The next morning came in thin and sour. A grey light soaked the horizon. The power still hadn't returned. Emil ate dry cereal out of a mug and drank lukewarm coffee boiled over a portable stove. The stone, still double-bagged, had frosted again, though the room was warmer now.

He logged the temperature by hand. Took another round of notes.

The skin on his fingers cracked when he flexed them. The air in the lab felt oddly dry despite the cold.

At noon, he tried the satellite phone. It wouldn't connect.

Not an error, just *blank*. No tone, no response. As if the signal wasn't down but simply didn't exist anymore.

He made his way to the post office near the edge of the dock, a squat building that leaned slightly into the wind. Inside, a woman in her fifties stood behind the counter, coat still on, gloves never removed.

She didn't ask what he wanted. "Nothing leaves this place once it's heard you," she said quietly. "Best you stop trying." Then she turned away and pretended to sort letters that hadn't arrived in weeks.

He stepped out onto the dock.

No boats in sight. No gulls. No tide swell.

The fjord looked painted.

Still.

Dead still.

And that music, the same faint hum he'd heard two nights before, was there again. Lower now. Coming not from the air, but *through* it. As if it were traveling through the water, the stone, the bones of the building itself.

He followed it back inside.

Emil stood in front of the sample tray, the hum of the lab equipment dull in the background, barely registering. The frost that had coated the outer surface of the bag had melted now, leaving behind a thin sheen of condensation. But the inside remained cold, unnaturally so. When he pressed a gloved finger to the plastic, a sharp sting pulsed up into his hand. It wasn't just chill; it was the dry, punishing cold of something that resisted the laws of ambient temperature. Something preserved by its own intent.

He leaned closer, squinting to examine the spiral carved into the object's surface. For a moment he was certain it had shifted, just slightly, a soft turn inward that hadn't been there before. He blinked, refocused. It had to be his eyes, or fatigue, or the refraction through the plastic. That's all it could be. Unless it wasn't.

He pulled the journal from Oslo out of the drawer, the one he'd received during the initial briefing. It was a partial translation, just a handful of copied pages from an old logbook dated sometime in the mid-1800s. He hadn't given it much attention, folklore and filler, he'd thought. A formality to pad out the archive. Now, with the stone in front of him and the temperature sinking around it like a tide withdrawing from shore, he opened the journal again.

On the third page, the image stopped him.

A drawing. A carved object. Smooth, worn edges, and at the centre, a spiral almost identical in scale and design to the one currently freezing the inside of his lab. Beneath the drawing, a line of handwriting marked the page, uneven, jagged ink scrawled as if it had been written in haste or with a trembling hand:

Hauet sang til oss. *The sea sang to us.*

He stared at the words for a long time. Beneath them, another phrase had been crossed out but remained partially visible if he tilted the paper toward the light.

Vi åpnet noe. *We opened something.*

He closed the journal, not quickly, but with the kind of deliberate motion meant to contain unease. Then he walked over to the freezer and locked the bagged stone inside, sealing it beneath two levels of stainless steel. It didn't matter that it was already cold. The act wasn't about preservation.

It was about distance. He just didn't want it near him anymore.

He checked the back room first, where the carcass had been stored under tarp and ice. Empty. No sign of drag, no damage. Just absence.

When he couldn't find it, he took the long path down to the water's edge, hoping somehow it had floated free.

The whale was gone.

There was no sign of it. No blood on the stones, no drag marks, no indication of where it might have floated. It hadn't broken up or washed out. It hadn't been taken. It had simply vanished, a hundred tons of flesh and bone erased without evidence or noise.

He stood for nearly twenty minutes, scanning the shoreline, eyes moving over every rise and hollow, trying to construct an explanation. Maybe the tide had shifted it free, though the currents weren't right for that. Maybe a boat, but no one in the village would have risked open water in weather like this, not at night, and certainly not without drawing attention.

He took the long path up along the ridge, hoping to catch a glimpse of current lines or anything that might indicate movement. Halfway along the trail, he found something worse.

A sliver of baleen, long and clean, sheared as if cut by something impossibly sharp. And next to it, a boot print.

It was deep. Facing the water. Just one.

He stared at the single print for a long time. He remembered the dive again. The blackout. The spiral. Maybe this was the second step of something that had started years ago.

There were no others.

No trail leading to or from it. As if the person who had left it had stepped forward into that exact place and either disappeared... or had never taken another step at all.

That night, the lights failed completely. Even the backup battery pack refused to charge.

He lit a candle, then another, setting them along the counters just to test the shadows. He told himself it was to maintain light, to create warmth. But what he was really doing was watching the way the flame behaved. Waiting for it to betray something.

And it did.

Not all the time, only when he turned his head too quickly, when the light caught the edge of a glass beaker or his reflection moved just slightly out of sync. Then he'd see it, the flicker bending in the wrong direction, as if the flame had followed a breath he hadn't taken.

He told himself it was the cold. Low oxygen. Thin air. He was tired. Overworked. Grasping at patterns that didn't belong.

But that night, he didn't sleep. Not even with the lights on.

Because sometime after two in the morning, a new sound joined the room.

It wasn't a knock. Not footsteps. It was breath. Low. Steady. Right at the threshold — not inside the room, but not entirely outside it either.

And it stayed there, just beyond the door, until dawn.

The Journal

That morning, Emil walked further than usual, past the last row of houses and toward a slope where a small chapel leaned into the wind. The paint had peeled, the windows boarded.

Inside, a man swept ash from the stone floor. Thin, bent slightly with age, his coat dusted with soot.

He didn't look up. Just said, "You shouldn't have opened it."

Emil paused.

"Opened what?"

The man nodded once toward the fjord. "The last one who did... he's in the bell."

Emil didn't ask what that meant. It was the drawer beneath the sink.

Old wood. Painted over more than once. Chipped where the paint had peeled, warped slightly at the edges. Emil had tried it the first day but assumed it was swollen shut. The rest of the drawers had come loose easily enough, all of them cluttered with rusted tools, empty sample bags, and half-used rolls of duct tape.

But this one was different.

He crouched down again now, staring at the thin red line of faded paint scrawled across its face, a cross, barely visible. Someone had pressed it into the surface with a fingertip while the paint was still drying. A warning, maybe. A seal.

And just above the handle, someone had written two words in heavy black pen:

DO NOT OPEN.

He stared at it for a long time.

The wind picked up outside, a rising hiss across the siding. He heard the soft thud of something shifting on the dock.

Then silence.

Emil gripped the handle. Pulled.

Nothing.

He wedged a flathead screwdriver between the drawer and frame, wiggled it gently. The wood groaned. He pried harder, slow, and deliberate. Something gave way with a soft crack. The drawer slid open.

Inside: a cloth-wrapped bundle, tied with twine. The cloth was brown with age, worn smooth like it had been folded and unfolded a hundred times. There was a smell, faint, but sharp. Not mildew. Not rot.

The stain had dried to a dark brown, somewhere between old ink and older blood. It had seeped into the folds of the cloth, stiffening the fibres and leaving a pattern like a fingerprint stretched thin across time. Emil hesitated for a moment, then reached into the crate and lifted the bundle out with both hands. The twine binding it snapped easily, brittle with age, giving way with a soft, papery crack that sounded louder than it should have in the stillness.

He unfolded the cloth slowly, layer by layer, revealing something that felt less like an object and more like a held breath. Inside was a journal.

The leather was blackened in places, weather-worn and rigid with moisture damage. The edges had curled inward as though the book had tried, at some point, to close itself. There was no title on the front, only a single, hand-burned mark: a circle crossed through the centre, not precisely drawn, but seared into the cover with deliberate force. It didn't feel decorative. It felt like a seal. Or a warning.

He turned it over in his hands, careful not to crack the spine further than time already had. The binding creaked as he opened it, releasing a faint scent, salt, dust, and something metallic beneath.

The pages inside were thin, yellowed at the edges, soft from years of damp and heat. But the writing remained dark, angled, carved into the paper with pressure and intent. It wasn't the hasty scrawl of a ship's log or the scratchings of someone trying to document while frightened. This had been written with purpose. With belief.

He turned to the first page.

It read:

Log of Captain Henrik Søreide
F/V Gåtestein
Lysefjord, Autumn, 1824

Emil turned the page and began to read.

October 12th.

The crew complains of unease. No wind, no sound, only still water and clouded sky. We are anchored but not tethered. I feel it in my bones, the fjord is listening.

October 14th.

Strange lights seen below the surface last night. Like lanterns, swinging slow, deep beneath us. Helvik claims he saw hands in the water, reaching. I beat him for drunkenness. But I saw them too.

October 15th.

We trawled this morning. Net brought up something solid. Thought it a bone at first. But it was carved. Runed. Smooth as river glass. The men begged me to toss it over. I did not.

October 17th.

Anders tore his eyes out. Said he could see it everywhere. The stone. In his dreams. Behind the water. He lived five hours. Screamed for most of it

Emil's hands tightened around the book, He turned the page.

The ink was darker here. Thicker. Letters began to wobble, as if the writer's hand had lost discipline.

October 19th.

The sea has gone wrong. It is not water now. It is skin. I do not sleep. I have heard singing in my sleep for days. They will not stop.

The stone was not meant to return. It seals something. Or it did.

The sea is different now. It has a face.

Emil closed the journal. His fingers were cold, trembling slightly. The building creaked behind him, nothing out of the ordinary. But the sound now carried weight. Like footsteps. Pauses. Waiting.

He placed the journal gently on the desk and reached for the cloth, intending to wrap it back up and return it to the crate, to fold the moment away and move on. But as his fingers touched the fabric, he froze.

There was a shape on the inside of the cloth now, faint, soft at the edges, still wet as though drawn in something that hadn't been there a moment earlier. A spiral. Not printed, not stitched, or pressed. It hadn't been added. It had *bled* through. The mark looked as if it had always been part of the cloth, waiting beneath the surface for the right time to rise.

For a long moment, he simply stared at it, unable to move. His thoughts went flat, not racing, just blank, a silence not born of calm but of refusal. The spiral wasn't decorative. It wasn't even expressive. It was revealing itself, piece by piece, like memory returning under pressure.

He stepped back, slowly at first, then sat hard in the chair without meaning to, the motion jarring the frame, the breath catching in his throat before it could fully leave his body. The air shifted.

The room felt tilted, not visually, not physically, but perceptually, as if space itself had leaned slightly in one direction, imperceptible but undeniable. Something was off-balance, and it wasn't just inside him.

The lights flickered once, a single dull flash across the lab walls, then died again with a soft mechanical sigh.

The silence that followed wasn't empty. It was full, heavy, close, and waiting.

Not the kind that came with power outages or snow. This was heavier. Fuller. Like the building was holding its breath around him. Emil stayed still in the chair, one hand resting on the journal's cracked leather cover, the other clenched tight in his lap.

The spiral on the cloth had faded now. Gone completely dry. No ink. No blood. No explanation.

He turned back to the journal, flipped forward.

The handwriting worsened as the pages went on, letters jittered, size fluctuated, margins collapsed. Like the captain had been writing during a storm, or something far more intimate: a breakdown.

October 20th.

I have seen the ship again. She drifts with no wind, no wake. A black sail, limp. Men on deck do not move. Do not breathe. But I feel their eyes. They wait. They wait for me.

Emil's stomach twisted.

That line, he'd written almost the same in his own log three nights ago, without realising. Something about the fjord, the silence. That sense of being watched.

He turned the page.

October 21st.

Voices now in the water. Singing in low tongue. I recognise my name. Not shouted. Whispered. I cannot find the stone. It moved on its own.

The men don't blink anymore. I cannot recall the last time one of them breathed.

Emil flipped again. Pages blurred.

October 23rd.

The sea speaks to itself. Below the hull. Like it forgot we were here.
We opened it.
And it saw us.

He didn't fully understand the words. But he knew the difference between metaphor and memory. And this felt like something remembered, just not by him.

Then the ink smeared, long black lines bleeding down the page like tears. But the next words were still readable. There is no way back. The fjord bends inward now. Every way leads deeper.

The water is not the door. It is the eye.

Emil sat back in the chair, breathing through his nose. The room was too still. No creak. No wind. Even the candle on the desk had stopped flickering.

He hadn't lit a candle.

That certainty landed in his chest like a dropped weight. His head turned slowly, not with panic, but with the heavy calculation of someone who already knows what they'll find.

In the far corner of the lab, near the sealed freezer, a candle burned quietly on the floor. Just one. Its flame stood tall but leaned slightly to the left, as if pushed by a breath that wasn't there. There was no draft. The room was sealed. Still.

His mouth went dry, and for a moment he didn't move. Then,

carefully. Almost reverently. He rose, taking care not to scrape the chair against the floor. Even so, each step sounded louder than it should have, echoing off the concrete like the room had grown deeper than before, like the space beneath his feet had stretched. Every footfall felt like a question.

He approached the candle.

The wax was still warm to the touch. The flame didn't flicker in his presence. It held steady, as though acknowledging him. And just beside the freezer door, nestled in the half-circle of its glow, was a single footprint, wet, bare, and unmistakably human.

The toes were long, uneven. The arch incomplete. But there were no prints leading toward it. No smudge of arrival. No trail of retreat. The print hadn't been made.

It had been *left*.

He turned, breath held tight in his chest and looked back to the desk.

The journal was gone.

Only the cloth remained, still folded neatly where he'd left it, but now soaked through, the centre darkened and heavy. He stepped back toward it slowly, hesitant but drawn. Kneeling, he reached out and unfolded the fabric, expecting the stone, bracing for it.

But it wasn't there.

Instead, tucked within the folds like a message placed in a ritual offering, was a single sheet of modern paper. White. Clean. Unmistakably fresh. Someone had slotted it there while he wasn't looking or while the room had distracted him.

The sentence at the centre was typed in a perfect, emotionless font.

"The sea did not forget. And neither will you."

He read it once. Then again.

And again.

He didn't need to understand it fully to believe it.

Dødningskipet

The man didn't want to talk at first.

He sat at the end of the dock with a pipe tucked in the corner of his mouth, unlit, hands too still for the cold. Wool layers wrapped him head to toe, more fisherman's ghost than man, eyes faded to the colour of sea worn rope. When Emil asked if he had a minute, the man said nothing. Just kept looking out across the fjord like he was waiting for something that hadn't shown yet.

Emil tried again. "I'm not with the police."

Still nothing.

"I just want to understand why the whales are dying. Why nobody wants to talk about what's in the water."

That got a twitch — barely. One corner of the old man's mouth folded in slightly, a crease appearing across the salt leather skin.

"You already know," the man said, still staring out at the water. "You just don't believe it yet."

"I'm trying to follow the facts."

"Facts don't float in Lysefjord," the old man replied. "They sink.

Same as everything else."

Emil hesitated, then sat down beside him, the edge of the dock damp and cold through his coat.

"Dødningskipet," he said quietly. "What is it?"

The man didn't look at him. Didn't blink.

"You don't say the name out loud," he muttered. "Not here. Not in fog."

"Why not?"

"Because it listens."

That landed in the air between them like a dropped net. Weighted and dense.

"It's just a story," Emil offered, gently.

"No." The word was flat. Final. "Just a memory."

He tapped the side of his head, then pointed out at the open water.

"You ever hear silence louder than a storm?"

Emil didn't answer.

The man didn't expect one.

"You hear singing in the fog?" he asked. "You leave. Doesn't matter what you're doing. Doesn't matter who you're with. You leave."

"Who's singing?"

"They are."

The man finally turned then. Looked directly at Emil for the first time. Eyes milky but sharp.

"They don't want to come back," he said. "But the stone calls them."

And then, softer:

"Don't whistle. Not even by accident."

Emil waited, hoping for more. But the man went quiet again.

Just raised the pipe to his lips, though he never lit it.

They sat in silence until the wind shifted, and the mist started rolling in.

The man stood up without another word and walked off the dock, slow but sure footed, disappearing into the grey.

Emil remained on the dock long after the man had disappeared. He wasn't sure why. The mist hadn't yet thickened, but the light had changed, subtly, almost imperceptibly, like something had shifted behind the clouds rather than within them. The horizon blurred at the edges. The air felt denser. Sound travelled strangely now, dull and elastic, as if the water had risen into the trees.

He watched the place where the old man had vanished, expecting movement, or a voice, or even a silhouette to re-emerge through the grey.

Nothing.

The pipe had never been lit. The man had never said his name.

Emil turned back toward the station slowly, boots dragging slightly across the damp wood. The cold didn't bite now, it pressed. It felt *thick*, like being submerged without realising he'd left the surface.

By the time he reached the door, mist had begun to settle into the folds of his coat. Not beads of moisture, **film**. Thin. Silken. Clinging. He brushed it off with the back of his sleeve, but it resisted. Not fully wet. Not fully dry.

Inside, the lab was still. He stood at the window, staring out as the treeline began to fade in sections, not vanishing all at once, but disappearing piece by piece, like memory eroding in reverse.

A sound crackled from the vent. He turned, but it stopped. Just heat pressure, maybe. Just shifting metal. But the silence that followed didn't feel like absence.

It felt like waiting.

By afternoon, the fog hadn't lifted.

It had thickened.

It didn't creep or slide or float, it hung, heavy and full. It wrapped itself around the station like an anchor chain. Emil watched it from the lab window, watched the trees blur, and vanish, watched the shore shrink down to a strip of wet stone.

He flipped on the emergency radio. Static. Adjusted the frequency. More static. Then something faint beneath it.

A note.

One, long, low note, almost too deep to hear.

He adjusted again.

Now voices.

Distant. Soft. Multilayered. Singing, but not melody. Something slower. He strained to catch words, but there were none. Just cadence. Chant without origin.

He shut the radio off.

Left it off.

By dusk, the fog swallowed everything.

Even the water.

Emil stood outside on the dock, jacket zipped tight, fingers deep in his pockets. The air had gone slick and salty, not briny like ocean salt — heavier, iron tanged.

He squinted.

Out in the fog, something shifted. It wasn't the slow heave of a wave or the soft diffusion of mist, this was different. A shape had formed where there had been only air and light. Dark. Tall. Low in the water. A silhouette that hadn't been there a moment ago and now refused to disappear.

Emil leaned forward slightly, holding his breath without meaning to, eyes narrowed, every muscle quiet. There were no lights, no engine sounds, no creak of hull or moan of rope. Nothing moved. But the shape continued to gain form. Not quickly. Not dramatically. Just slowly enough that it no longer felt imagined. As if the fog had decided it was time to show him something.

It was a ship.

Old. Wooden. Weathered and tall.

Its sails were down, sagging like wet cloth, and the hull bore cracks that ran deep into its structure, as though it had come from a place far older than this sea. But it didn't move. It didn't drift or cut through the water like a vessel meant to travel. It simply existed there, fixed in place, not docked or anchored but present in a way that felt deliberate.

Watching.

He could see more now, the masts rising like skeletal limbs, the lines of rigging slack and swaying despite the stillness in the air. The ship carried no flag, no signal, no sign of allegiance or purpose. No wake disturbed the water around it.

But Emil knew. Absolutely and without doubt, that he was being watched. Not by something from the shore. Not by the hills or the trees or the sky. He was being observed from that ship. Studied. Remembered.

The singing began again, but it no longer came from the radio or any machine. It was emerging from the water itself. Low and resonant, shaped like a voice that had never needed lungs.

Emil stepped backward without realising it, his foot hitting the frame of the door behind him with a soft, jarring thud. The impact startled him into stillness, as though his body had moved before his mind could decide whether to run or kneel.

The wind did not rise. The fog did not shift. The night remained suspended, not in peace, but in stillness.

And the ship?

And it hadn't moved.

Emil slammed the door shut behind him.

The sound of the latch clicking into place shouldn't have felt like relief, but it did. He stood there with one hand braced on the wall, heart thudding hard enough to make his ribs ache. The singing was gone — or maybe the walls had simply swallowed it.

He waited.

Listened.

Nothing but the soft hum of the power system cycling — generator finally holding steady. The lab light flickered once, then held.

He crossed quickly to the desk and powered up the digital recorder. It had been running when he stepped outside — clipped to his coat like always, the red-light blinking. A safety habit from field work, meant to capture thoughts on the fly. Now, it felt like a line in the sand. Something that could prove what he'd seen.

He hit playback.

At first: silence.

Then footsteps. His voice, steady but uncertain. Notes about the weather. The fog. Time stamp just before dusk.

Then the shift.

That was his voice. Clear, composed, observational. The tone he always used when documenting. But then something shifted in the background, barely audible at first. A faint hum began to rise beneath his words, subtle and low, the kind of sound that sits just under breath. It might have been interference. Might have been equipment noise.

But then it changed.

The hum began to swell, not louder exactly, but denser, like pressure building in a room where nothing had moved. Emil's voice faltered mid-sentence. Not trailed off, not interrupted. It simply stopped. Cut off clean. No breath, no pause, no click.

It was replaced by something else.

A slow inhale, long and deliberate, followed by a thick, muffled exhale. Wet at the edges, as if someone were breathing through water, pressed directly against the microphone. It wasn't mechanical. It wasn't looped.

Emil froze in place.

He scrubbed forward a few seconds, uncertain if what he'd heard had been real or imagined. The breathing continued. Unbroken. Steady. It followed its own rhythm, slow and deliberate, too deep to be his own. Too weighted. Too intimate.

Then came the whisper.

Not words, not language, just breath twisted into the shape of sound. Like a throat trying to speak through memory instead of muscle. It sent a pulse of static across the waveform, but no pattern followed. Just that whisper.

And then, just as suddenly, silence.

His voice never returned to the recording.

He played it back again, this time with the volume lowered. The result was the same. His observation faded, replaced by the sound of someone. Or something. Listening *back*.

It wasn't a glitch. The file was intact. His voice had simply... ceased.

He leaned back in the chair, hands curled around the edge of the desk.

The cold in the room wasn't from the weather anymore.

It came from inside the station. From below the floorboards. From the walls.

He looked out the window again, half expecting the silhouette to be closer.

But there was only fog now.

Heavy and still.

Like a closed mouth.

He didn't bother trying to sleep.

Instead, he backed up the audio file, burned a copy to a drive, and scribbled the time and content into the margin of the journal he'd begun to keep for himself. Not for work. Just to hold something still.

Around 3 a.m., the fog outside shifted.

Not cleared, just pulled away, like something had passed through it.

He turned off the light and stood at the window again.

The water shone with moonlight. Silver and flat. No ripples.

But out on the shoreline, he saw something else.

Footprints.

a set of prints in the snow.

They began halfway up the bank, not at the road or the ridge or any clear path, but right in the untouched slope, as if whoever or whatever, had made them had appeared mid-step. There was no trail leading to them, no signs of approach, no disruption in the surrounding drifts. Just clean, deliberate impressions pressed into the snow like memory shaped by weight.

He studied them, heart knocking once hard against his ribs. The spacing was too wide for any person. Each step landed farther apart than a normal gait would allow. The depth was wrong too, pressed deep into the snowpack, far deeper than the weight of a human foot should have registered, even with force.

And they led directly to the lab door.

Emil stepped back without thinking, then took another half-step, his breath suddenly sharper in his chest. He didn't turn away from the prints. Didn't want to lose sight of them. But his hand reached behind him instinctively, fingers curling around the freezer handle.

Without taking his eyes off the doorway, he opened it.

The cold air rolled out in a shallow wave. Inside, the bagged stone still sat exactly where he'd left it, resting in its metal tray, sealed in thick plastic.

It hadn't moved.

But something had changed.

The spiral etched into its surface looked deeper now, not eroded or worn, but *recarved*. As though someone had pressed into it again with fresh force, deepening the groove, sharpening the edge. It looked deliberate. It looked new. Not like time had shaped it. Like intention had.

With his other hand, Emil slowly pushed the freezer door shut.

Then locked it.

He didn't know if the lock mattered anymore.

But the gesture made him feel like it might.

Even if only for another night.

At first light, Emil stepped outside into air that felt too still to belong to morning. The fog had lifted sometime during the night, not burned off or pushed away by wind, but simply absent now, as if it had finished whatever it came to do.

The ship was gone.

No silhouette on the water, no lines of mast or trace of wake. The fjord lay flat and undisturbed, as if nothing had ever risen from it.

But in the distance, high on the ridge above the treeline, something stood. A dark figure, tall, unmoving, watching the water.

It didn't pace or shift its weight. It didn't retreat. It stood fixed against the sky, so still it almost disappeared into the rock and snow. Almost. But not quite. Emil saw it, and he knew, without needing confirmation, that it saw him too.

There was no sign of recognition, no movement of hand or limb. Just stillness. The kind that belonged to something considering its next motion carefully. Slowly. As if it hadn't yet decided whether to descend.

As if it was waiting to be remembered.

Carving

The whale hadn't drifted far.

Emil found it again the next morning, washed into a narrow rocky inlet two miles north of the station. The current must've carried it there during the night, like the fjord had tried to return what it had taken.

It lay at an angle against the shore, half submerged, the water around it glassy and strangely dark. A few gulls circled above but didn't land. They screeched once or twice, then left altogether.

He waded through the shallows, boots crunching through silt and loose stone, and reached the carcass with the morning still low behind the ridge.

The skin was bloated more than before, the pale grey turning almost translucent. It looked unreal in the cold light, not dead, not alive, just wrong.

He crouched beside it, set down his pack, and unzipped the canvas with frozen fingers.

It was supposed to be routine. Quick incision. Internal recheck. See if the stomach had expanded or split. Confirm if anything was still inside.

He slipped the blade between the rib seam and slid downward, slow, and careful. The tissue parted easily, too easily. The stomach lining was loose, like something had softened it from the inside out.

He reached in.

And froze.

His hand hit something solid. Small. Not bone.

Round. Smooth.

He grabbed it and pulled.

A carved object came free, grey stone slick with fluid, streaked with blood and silt. It slipped from his glove into the water and hit the rock with a dull clack. He knelt, heart thudding, and turned it over.

A spiral.

Not like the one from before.

The same.

Exactly the same. Even the small fracture line that cut through the edge of the spiral, healed smooth and white like scar tissue.

It was impossible.

He stood motionless, eyes fixed on the object resting in the tray, breath fogging the glass in short, shallow bursts. His body was trying to regulate itself, but his mind refused to follow. He had sealed the first one, the original stone, in the freezer hours ago, locked it behind two layers of containment. He had heard the latch click. Had watched the temperature gauge fall. He knew, with absolute certainty, that the object had not left its containment.

And yet here it was again.

Identical. Unmarked. Sitting in the open, as if placed there deliberately. As if it had returned, not moved, not transported, but followed.

Unless it wasn't an object at all.

Unless it didn't need to be carried to arrive.

Unless it had always been one step behind him.

His hand moved without full consent, reaching forward slowly, fingers wrapping around the smooth edges with the familiar dread of muscle memory. The moment his skin made contact, a sound rose in the back of his awareness, not external, not environmental.

It was whispering.

Soft at first. Almost imagined.

But it wasn't a hallucination. And it wasn't coming from the room.

It was his voice.

Low and steady. Muttering words he couldn't quite parse, threading themselves around the base of his skull like static given breath. His mouth remained closed. He was certain of that. And yet the whisper continued, shaped in his own cadence, his own tone, as though some deeper part of him had begun speaking without waiting for permission.

And it wasn't going to stop.

He heard it clearly, not just in his ears, but inside his skull.

His voice, repeated, low, and breathy, saying a phrase he didn't understand, syllables mangled, ancient, but somehow still his.

He dropped the stone.

Staggered back.

The sound stopped instantly.

He knelt on the rock, panting, and touched the side of his face.

Wet.

He brought his hand to his face, instinctively, uncertain whether the sting behind his ear was real or imagined. When he looked down at his fingers, they came away wet. Streaked with blood. Thin, watery. A slow trail leaking from just below his left ear.

He wiped again, slower this time. More blood surfaced, glistening along the ridgeline of his jaw. It wasn't flowing fast, but it was steady. Controlled. As though something inside his head had split, not from trauma, but from pressure. Like a seam opening slowly from within.

Something inside him was bleeding.

He turned toward the water, not out of fear, but out of instinct, as if it had asked him to look. The fjord was still. Completely motionless. It reflected the sky in a thin, perfect sheet, too calm to trust. The surface didn't ripple. The wind didn't move it. And yet it felt alive.

It felt aware.

Watching.

The stone rested where he had found it, its spiral glistening faintly with mist, still warm, still waiting. This time, he didn't reach for it. Didn't claim it. He left it on the rock, untouched.

But as he turned and stepped away, legs unsteady beneath him, breath caught high in his chest, he realised the distance meant nothing. His coat clung to him, soaked through. His hands trembled. But the weight he carried now didn't come from cold or exhaustion.

He could feel it.

Not behind him, following in silence. Not ahead, waiting around the next bend.

It was inside him now.

Settled. Quiet.

And it wasn't gone. Only waiting, like a voice paused mid-sentence, held just behind the teeth, patient enough to wait until it was allowed to speak again.

Emil didn't remember the walk back.

One moment he was crouched beside the carcass, hands wet and shaking, blood in his ear. The next, he stood in the marine station's galley, jacket dripping onto the floor, breath catching in his throat.

He didn't even know how he'd gotten through the door. Or why his boots weren't on anymore.

He peeled off the soaked outer layer and moved to the mirror above the sink.

The bleeding had stopped, mostly. Just a red smear down the side of his neck. But when he looked closer, he saw something else. Something deeper.

The skin just behind his ear was *darker* now. Not bruised. Stained.

A thin spiral, almost invisible unless he tilted his head in just the right light. The lines weren't sharp, but they were real.

His skin had remembered the shape.

Even though he had left the stone behind.

He didn't log it.

Not right away.

Instead, he sat at his desk and opened the file folder the Oslo researcher had sent. The one that started all this. Inside was the printed photograph, grainy and faded, of a carved stone found years ago near Torridon.

He laid it flat under the lamp.

Spiral. Fracture. Same shape, same angle.

He had seen this photo before. But now something was different.

Below the photo, where the label had once read *"Artifact #3, recovered Scotland"*, something new had appeared, handwritten in pencil:

"Return it."

But that wasn't the strangest part.

The handwriting was his.

He knew it.

Same way he knew how he dotted his lowercase *i*'s. Slightly right leaning, faint pressure at the end of each stroke. He even recognised the faint ink smudge where his palm must've brushed the note as he wrote it.

Except he hadn't.

He would remember.

Wouldn't he?

He stood, too fast, chair legs scraping the concrete.

His head swam, the hum again, faint, distant, but there.

He walked to the freezer and opened it.

The first stone sat where he left it, inside the double bag. Still sealed. Still cold.

He stared at it. Then back at the desk.

Two identical stones.

Miles apart.

One sealed. One abandoned.

But somehow… connected.

Or worse. *Not separate at all.*

Maybe the stone wasn't a single object.

Maybe it was a shape the world remembered how to make.

A *summoning*, not a thing.

The radio crackled behind him.

He turned. Stepped over to it. Flicked the receiver to channel four the local band. No reason. Just habit.

Static.

Then, from somewhere deep within the static. Barely audible at first, came a single tone.

It was low, stretched and thin, resonating like wind through hollow wood or bone, not musical, not rhythmic, but shaped in a way that suggested memory. Not something heard, but something remembered *wrong*.

And then his voice emerged from the noise.

"Return it."

Two words. Crisp. Flat.

Except it wasn't his voice now. Not *him*, speaking in this moment. It was a recording, one he hadn't made, or didn't remember making. The inflection was right. The tone matched. But the cadence was off, slightly bent at the edges, as if warped by time or tape or distance.

The phrase repeated.

"Return it."

Each repetition brought a slight distortion. First the pitch wavered, then the timing. The words began to drag. Elongate. As though the recording itself had become tired of its own command, stretching the syllables into something between breath and demand.

By the third loop, Emil wasn't certain if it was still a recording or if the voice had moved on to speak directly again.

Over and over:

"Return it."

"Return it."

"Return it."

He switched the radio off.

And stood in the middle of the room, alone, air thin and crackling.

The spiral behind his ear itched.

Or pulsed. Or both.

That night, he didn't try to sleep.

He didn't even dim the lights.

He sat with the journal on his lap and re read the captain's final entries.

The stone moved again. It was not carried. It was not found. It was placed.

I believe now it remembers more than we do. It knows what we forgot.

The final entry wasn't dated. Just one line:

I hear myself before I speak.

Surface Tension

They started showing up in the early hours, just before the first break of light.

Not with a sound, not all at once.

Just one at first. Then another.

Figures, standing ankle deep in the fjord.

Facing the station.

Not moving.

Not blinking.

Emil first thought they were shadows, tricks of fog and early light. But shadows don't stay when the sun rises. These did.

He stood at the window with a mug of cold coffee in his hand, staring down at the shore. Two of them, spaced apart like sentries. Barefoot. Their clothes waterlogged, heavy. Faces pale. Heads tilted slightly too far, like something inside had forgotten how to hold them upright.

They didn't watch. They waited. Not to be seen, but to see who was still pretending they couldn't. He stepped back from the glass, slowly, and turned off the light behind him.

When he looked again, they were still there.

A third one now.

Closer to the dock.

That morning, Emil walked into the village under a sky that refused to shift. The clouds hung low and unmoving, heavy and colourless, the air dense with cold that didn't bite so much as press inward. Overhead, the sky had turned the colour of dirty ice, thick, impassive, the kind of light that flattened the landscape into shadowless grey.

He passed the same houses he always did, their windows fogged from within, their curtains drawn just a little too tightly. No one waved. No one called out. One door slammed shut as he approached, fast and hard enough to rattle the frame. Behind another, a woman yanked the curtain closed with one hand, her other resting on the shoulder of a child who stared through the glass a moment longer before vanishing with her.

The shop was empty. Not just quiet, but hollow, the kind of quiet that made sound feel inappropriate. Even the shelves looked different now, sparsely stocked, half-forgotten. Not recently picked over, but long neglected, as if the act of restocking had become irrelevant. A small radio sat behind the counter, hissing out a stream of low static, broken occasionally by what might have been a word or just a glitch in the signal.

He waited ten minutes.

No one came to the till.

Eventually, he left without buying anything.

On the way back, he saw the old fisherman again, the one who had warned him, days ago, not to whistle. The man stood exactly where Emil remembered him, posture unchanged, face unreadable beneath the brim of a hat crusted with salt and old rain. This time, the man didn't speak.

He didn't even move.

He just stared as Emil passed, not with judgment or fear, but with the quiet gaze of someone watching a boat slip out of view, as if he already knew how far Emil had gone, and was waiting only to see whether he would return.

The wind shifted before Emil reached the station.

He smelled it first, the sharp tang of salt rolling through the trees like a warning. Stronger than before. Stronger than it should've been at this distance from the shore. It wasn't just on the air. It was *in* the air now, clinging to his coat, his throat, lining the back of his teeth like something he'd swallowed in sleep.

When he stepped inside, the silence of the lab greeted him not with stillness, but with anticipation. The lights buzzed faintly overhead, just enough to remind him they could go out again at any time.

Then he saw the journal.

It was open on the desk, laid flat, perfectly centred, the spine spread to a page he didn't remember turning to. He hadn't left it that way. He was sure of it. The ink on the page looked too sharp. Too clean. Not the captain's hand, not the faded strokes of a weathered logbook.

This page had been typed. Recently.

Just five lines:

> The drowned don't need air.
>
> They just need eyes.
>
> And yours are open.
>
> Keep them that way.
>
> We're nearly through.

He picked up the page with shaking fingers. It wasn't part of the original binding, the paper was clean, printer stock white, slotted in carefully.

He checked the printer first, half-expecting it to still be warm, but the machine was dark. No blinking lights. No hum. When he pressed the power button, nothing happened. The log displayed no recent jobs. It was as if it had never been used.

Next, he opened the desk drawers, unsure what he was looking for until he found it. Another page. Waiting.

Typed.

Same font. Same spacing. Same absence of explanation. No heading. No signature.

Just a sentence:

You looked at them. That's enough.

He stared at the words longer than he meant to, trying to convince himself that he didn't understand them, but he did. There was no mistaking the implication. It hadn't asked anything of him. It hadn't demanded. It had simply acknowledged what had already happened.

Looking was permission.

He turned toward the window again, slowly this time, not with urgency but with inevitability.

There were four figures now.

One stood on the rocky shore, its shape partially obscured by mist. Another stood just at the waterline, feet planted where the tide would have kissed the stones a few hours earlier. Two more waited on the dock, still, precise, and facing him directly. Their postures didn't waver. Their forms were too far to see in detail, but their presence was unmistakable.

Then, without rush or force, their heads turned.

All four at once.

Not fast. Not violent. But with the weight of intention. Not to intimidate, but to let him know that whatever barrier had existed between him and them was now gone.

They had seen him. And now he had seen them.

That night, the generator failed.

Not sputtered. Not strained. It simply died, as though it had chosen to stop.

No hum. No lights. No heat.

Just the lab returning to its most natural state: quiet, cold, and watched.

The silence was so complete he could hear his own pulse behind his eyes.

He sat with the pages on the table in front of him, six of them now.

All written in the same clinical formatting, like they'd been copied from a report he hadn't written yet.

One of them was a description of himself, what he was wearing, where he was standing, even what mug was in his hand.

All accurate.

All written in past tense.

He tried the satellite phone again.

Nothing.

He turned on the backup recorder. Clicked to playback.

"This is Dr. Emil Strand. Lysefjord station. I'm documenting… sightings. Phenomena."

His voice stammered.

"They appear to be. People. At least, were people. Now they just, watch."

Click.

He paused it.

Then played it again.

But this time, the words had changed.

It was still his voice, same cadence, same breath pattern, the same flat tone he always used during field notes. But the content was different now. He hadn't said these things. Not aloud. Not intentionally. And yet the words unfurled with calm certainty, like a memory returning not to be questioned, but obeyed.

"They never drowned. Not really. They were taken. Submerged and remembered."

"The spiral is not a symbol. It's an opening. A slow turn toward something older."

Each sentence arrived like it had always been waiting inside him, waiting for permission. Not discovery. Not translation. Just *acknowledgement.*

Emil lunged forward and shut off the recorder, stabbing at the button with too much force. He yanked the batteries from the back with shaking hands and flung the device across the room. It struck the far wall and fell to the floor with a hollow thud, skidding slightly before coming to rest near the edge of the desk.

But the voice didn't stop.

It had never been in the machine.

It continued in his head, soft now, almost tender, like it no longer needed to raise its volume to be heard. The words pulsed behind his eyes, behind his ears, somewhere deeper than thought. Not shouted. Not urgent.

Just patient.

It wasn't trying to convince him.

It was waiting for him to catch up.

The voice had begun repeating a name, one Emil didn't recognise. It came softly at first, layered in static, then grew clearer, sharper, as if the recorder had never truly been off.

Without thinking, he tore the page from the journal and struck a match from the emergency kit tucked beneath the sink. The flame caught quickly, curling up the corner of the paper. But the way it burned felt wrong. The scent wasn't right, not paper, not ink. No smoke. No ash. The fire consumed it silently, folding the page inward on itself like it was erasing more than surface. Like it was erasing weight. Memory. Presence.

And then it was gone.

For a moment, Emil let himself believe that mattered. That it had worked. His breath eased slightly, the tremor in his hands settled, and he turned back toward the desk, eyes drawn to the space where the journal had been.

But he stopped cold.

There was another page.

Not from the journal. Not handwritten. Just lying there in the open drawer as if it had always been waiting for him to look. The paper was identical, same weight, same type. The edges were clean. The text centred and precise.

You looked at them. That's enough.

The font was typed. Not printed by the lab's machine, the printer hadn't powered on in over two days. And yet the page was fresh. Still warm to the touch, like it had come straight off a press that didn't exist.

His name was at the top:

DR. EMIL STRAND - LOG 6: ACCEPTANCE

You burned the message. That was part of it.

You wanted to forget. We let you.

But now we will remember for you.

He slammed his fist against the desk, scattering his notes, the journal, a cracked mug. The page fluttered but didn't fall.

His ears rang with pressure, a rising hiss, like the air in the station had thickened.

Then came the knock.

Except it wasn't a knock. Not really.

It was softer than that, a slow, deliberate pressure against the back door. Not forceful. Not even insistent. Just a touch. As if fingers had rested there for a moment, testing the space between presence and entry.

Once.

Then again.

He didn't move. Didn't speak. His body remained still, but something inside him had already shifted, some unspoken understanding forming just below thought.

The third touch brought a faint scraping sound. It wasn't loud, but it lingered, the kind of noise that stuck in the teeth. Fingernail, maybe. Knuckle. Or wet wood dragging lightly against the frame. Something tactile. Intimate. Like whatever was outside knew the shape of the door.

He stood up and walked toward it, not quickly, not cautiously, but with a strange kind of detachment, as though approaching the signature on a contract he didn't remember signing and couldn't stop from being submitted.

He stopped at the threshold.

Stared at the handle.

Didn't touch it.

Instead, he turned away and crossed back to the desk, his limbs moving in a rhythm that no longer felt entirely his. Another page waited there.

Typed.

Not warm this time.

But signed.

And the signature was his.

He recognised the uneven loop in the "S," the long, dragging downstroke in the "d" tiny flourishes no one else would know to fake. But he hadn't written it. Not that he remembered. Still, he didn't doubt its authenticity.

The message above the signature was brief:

They are not dead. You are just early.

He didn't scream. Didn't cry. His hands lowered gently into his lap as he sank into the chair, every motion quiet, deliberate, final. Outside the window, the figures had multiplied.

Seven now.

No longer lingering on the shoreline.

They stood at the base of the station stairs, arranged in silence, their silhouettes sharp in the fading light. They didn't move. Didn't shift. They didn't need to.

They were watching. Always watching.

And as the last thin edge of daylight drained from the fjord, the air inside the station began to change. The pressure wasn't directional, it came from everywhere at once, folding in on him like a closing palm. His skin tingled. The back of his neck flushed.

Then the spiral behind his ear began to itch again.

Not sharply. Not as pain. But as heat.

A low, steady warmth, slow and deep, like a brand, just beneath the surface, pulsing in time with something older than heartbeat.

He pulled his collar up without thinking, trying not to touch the mark. Trying not to speak. Trying not to look down at the new page that had just appeared on the desk, resting beside the last.

But it didn't matter.

He already knew what it said. He'd known before the letters were formed. Before the paper even existed.

He knew it by heart.

Let them in.

Witness

It began with water, not crashing in with force, but creeping, a thin, steady trickle sliding beneath the door, spreading across the floorboards in a quiet, deliberate crawl. Emil felt it before he saw it, dreamed it before he woke, cold water brushing across his ankles in a rising line that never rushed, only crept with purpose. The kind of cold that felt like memory, slow and certain.

Then he was standing.

But not in the station.

He was on a deck, aged wood beneath his feet, some boards bowed and softened by time, ropes curled near his boots like coiled serpents in sleep. Fog clung to the air like cloth, dense and unmoving, thick enough to taste. It didn't lift. It didn't roll. It simply was.

He glanced at his hands, bare, damp, skin pale as wax. The air around him carried a scent that wasn't just salt. It was older. Something like oil slicked over something rotting but not dead. Not quite. A wrongness beneath the surface.

He turned, expecting open sea.

But they were there.

Bodies. Not scattered or heaped. Arranged. Upright. Dozens of them, standing shoulder to shoulder with bowed heads, waterlogged hair clinging to motionless faces. Barefoot, silent, facing forward. They didn't seem aware of him, or maybe they did and simply chose not to react.

He moved among them.

Careful. Quiet.

None stirred. Some bore wounds, mouths torn as if stretched too far, hands whittled to bone, not by violence, but erosion. One figure had a rope hanging loosely from his neck, not tied, just draped, like a symbol carried, not worn.

They didn't breathe.

But they waited.

At the centre of the ship, there was no helm. No mast. Just a low, open deck, and beyond it, a narrow stairwell descending into darkness. A mouth carved from shadow.

He didn't want to go down.

But he already was.

The steps beneath his feet changed with each descent—wood gave way to stone, slick with condensation, ancient in a way that didn't just suggest age, but history forgotten. Carved in a slow spiral, the stair narrowed with every turn, coiling downward like a thought burrowing deeper into the mind. Beams loomed low overhead, some so close he had to duck, the air thickening around him with every step.

The walls were etched.

Runes, faint, and crude, burned into the stone in a language that felt more rhythmic than readable. Among them: the spiral, repeating again and again. Not drawn, etched with intention. One pulsed faintly as he passed, a heartbeat in stone.

The silence here was total.

Only his footsteps remained, echoing too long, too loud, as though the stairwell had been waiting years to hear them again. Water ran down the walls, slow as breath, never pooling, just traveling.

Then came a voice, quiet, familiar.

His own.

It didn't echo. It wasn't behind him, or above, or drifting from the dark. It was beside him, level with his ear, as though walking just out of sight.

Soft. Steady. Certain.

"You were always part of it."

He didn't turn. He couldn't. Every part of him understood that looking would be a mistake.

The stair ended without ceremony.

And the chamber opened like an inhale held too long. No ceiling. No walls he could see. Just space.

At the centre, a mirror.

It stood without frame or base, an impossible shape, held by nothing, and yet there. The surface was black, still as oil.

He approached.

And the mirror came to life.

Not with reflection, but memory.

Him. Standing on the dock.

But he wasn't alone.

One of the drowned was beside him. A hand rested on Emil's shoulder, gently. No violence. No force. Just contact, familiar and quiet.

In the image, Emil did not recoil.

He smiled.

He woke gasping, the image of the mirror still stamped behind his eyes, breath catching like he'd surfaced from somewhere too deep. Sheets clung damp to his skin. The station was dark again, no buzz from the overheads, no familiar clatter from the generator. Just stillness.

And the floor was wet.

He swung his legs over the edge of the bunk and stepped into water. Not deep, an inch, maybe less, but cold and unmistakably salt. No storm. No leak. Just seawater, drawn in from nowhere, creeping outward like it had found its way home.

The trail led him down the hallway.

Past the dark windows, past the lab door, until he reached the freezer. The one he'd sealed. Locked.

It still hummed, just barely, its light a dull glow in the gloom. But above it, carved into the wall with fresh gouges that hadn't been there the day before, was another spiral.

This one was deeper. Crude but precise, lines overlapping in a way that suggested pressure, not haste. The edges were still wet.

And beneath it, scrawled in ragged block letters:

YOU'VE SEEN.

He didn't remember carving it.

But the shape, he recognised it the way you recognise your own name in a crowd. Not a symbol. Not anymore. Something closer to a fingerprint.

He took a step back, breath shallow, the weight of the mirror still pressing against his thoughts. Turning toward the freezer, he moved as if underwater, each motion careful, unwilling to break whatever thin layer of calm remained in the room. His fingers found the latch, cold and stiff beneath his grip, and he hesitated for just a moment before releasing it with a soft click.

The lid lifted slowly.

Inside, the stone sat exactly where he'd left it, but it wasn't the same.

Not entirely.

It had changed.

What had once been smooth, and shallow had deepened. The centre had started to bore inward, a depression forming like the first turn of a drill. Its surface shimmered faintly, not wet, but alive, as if something beneath it was moving at a molecular crawl.

Then it pulsed.

Just once.

He touched the outer bag with his fingertips.

The whisper returned.

This time it wasn't in his ears or his skull. It was somewhere in between, a place he didn't have a word for. His jaw clenched. His throat tightened. And without willing it, he felt his lips part, breath shaping syllables he didn't understand.

He snapped the lid shut. Relocked the seal.

The whisper stopped.

He stood in the hallway, hand still clenched around the freezer latch, the whisper lingering like an afterimage in his breath. His pulse hadn't slowed. It had simply changed, settled into a new rhythm, one that didn't feel entirely his.

Then a sound.

Not a bang. Not a crash.

Just a creak. Soft. Slow. Measured.

A floorboard.

He turned toward the bunk room, steps light, careful on the slick floor.

The water had spread farther now, no longer pooling but trailing beneath doorframes like veins. He pushed the door open.

Nothing.

No one.

But the mirror was fogged.

He hadn't touched it. Hadn't even looked at it in days.

Yet it was clouded now, streaked faintly as though someone had leaned in close face pressed just inches from the glass. Closer than breath. Like they'd been watching him sleep.

He moved toward the mirror, each step drawn out as if the air had thickened around him. When he reached the glass, he wiped the surface with the flat of his hand, clearing away the fog in a slow, deliberate arc.

His reflection emerged, but something about it felt... off. It stared back, yes, but lagged by the barest breath, half a heartbeat too slow, like it was thinking before it acted.

He raised his hand, testing the image.

The reflection copied him, but with a hesitation, like a puppet waiting for its cue.

Then it smiled.

Not broadly. Not grotesquely. Just a small, uneven curl of the lips on one side of the mouth, a gesture that felt too knowing to dismiss. It was the kind of smile that didn't ask permission to exist.

Emil stood still, every instinct urging him not to flinch.

The reflection didn't hold back.

It blinked, once, too slow, too deliberate and then opened its mouth.

No sound came out.

Only the pressure, sudden and sharp, like his ears had dropped below pressure depth in an instant. He staggered, breath caught mid-chest, a reflex long out of his control.

But pressure filled Emil's ears, an impossible weight, like water rushing in from the inside out. He staggered, stumbled back into the table behind him.

A candle fell somewhere behind him.

He didn't see it drop, only heard the dull clink as it rolled across the floorboards, slow and deliberate, like it knew exactly where to stop. It came to rest a few feet away, then settled upright, still burning.

He stared at it for a long moment.

He hadn't lit it. He hadn't brought it into the room. There were no matches nearby, no fuel. And yet, there it was, flame steady, tall, casting a shadow that stretched unnaturally across the wall. The shape it threw bent subtly as it moved, curving at the edges in a direction the light shouldn't have allowed. Like the flame was answering to something else entirely.

He didn't look back.

Didn't close the door behind him.

He just stepped away, out of the room, walking without urgency but also without will, as if his body had surrendered the need for questions.

Back at the desk, the journal lay open again. He hadn't left it that way. The spine had shifted. The pages had turned. A new sheet had been added to the middle, clean, crisp, the paper still resisting the air slightly. The ink was wet. It smelled fresh.

But it wasn't a log. Not data. Not notes.

This was a message.

> *This is where the change completes.*
> *Where you are no longer observing.*
> *Where you become part of the pattern.*

The spiral turns inward.

He took a step back, breath catching, but his eyes were already drawn to the floor, another page waited there, lying flat near the base of the desk, as if it had been placed gently, deliberately.

He bent to pick it up, his hands trembling now, the motion slow and reluctant.

This one wasn't typed.

It had been written by hand, the strokes neat and deliberate, with a slight slant. Not rushed. Not copied. Personal. But it wasn't his handwriting.

And yet, it was signed.

Dr. Malcolm Bryce.

He stared at the name, heart skipping once. The finality of it arrived before his thoughts could keep up. Then he read the line beneath it.

One last message. Small. Tucked at the bottom like a closing whisper.

If you find this, they've already chosen you.
They chose me too.

Collapse

The whales kept coming.

By the end of the week, four more had washed up. Two minkes, one calf, and what Emil suspected was a juvenile fin. All found in different parts of the fjord, all dead without obvious cause. No propeller damage. No infection. No parasites.

Just silence in their organs.

That's what the autopsies showed. Lungs intact but unused. Brains grey with inactivity, like they had shut down before death, like they'd willed themselves out.

Emil stopped cataloguing them properly after the third. His notes became fragmented — short bursts in the margin of his journal, clipped audio files that cut off mid-sentence. He couldn't focus. The station was no longer a safe shell against the wild. It had become something else. An echo chamber. And it was amplifying the wrong things.

The morning the fin whale came ashore, Anja went missing.

She'd been assisting from Bergen, meant to stay only three days.

Mostly paperwork. Basic sampling. She hadn't wanted to come at all, no one did, but she'd agreed to a short field stint before returning to her lab.

That morning, Emil had woken to find her bed neatly made, duffel gone.

She hadn't signed out. There was no entry in the logbook, no message, no alert. No boat had arrived or departed that morning. The dock was undisturbed. Her coat still hung by the door, exactly where she always left it, sleeves empty, hood slightly damp from the night before.

At first, Emil assumed she'd gone into the village, restless, maybe irritated after the last few days of tension. He imagined her taking the trail through the trees, needing distance, needing quiet. But by nightfall, when no one had seen her and no calls came through, that assumption began to crack.

Her phone was still charging on the galley counter, screen dark, untouched since the night before. Her backpack sat by her bunk, half-zipped, a book inside opened to the middle. No signs of preparation. No intent to leave. Just absence, pure and sudden.

The back door had been left slightly open.

Not wide. Not broken. Just open enough to let in the cold. A narrow gap between warmth and winter, barely noticeable, unless you were looking for what had passed through it.

And near her bunk, on the pale floorboards, he saw it.

A single footprint.

Small. Bare. Wet.

It faced inward.

There were no matching prints. No trail leading away. No muddy heel. Just that one, toes pointed toward the bed, like someone had stepped inside. Not searching. Not wandering. Just *entering*.

She hadn't walked out.

Something had walked in.

That night, Emil didn't sleep. And after that, he stopped trying altogether.

He sat by the window at night, eyes raw, breath visible even indoors. His journal filled with crossed out lines, looped phrases, numbers he didn't remember recording. Every few hours he'd walk the perimeter of the station, flashlight in hand, checking for tracks.

They never led anywhere.

Just appeared.

Then vanished.

One morning, he found one on the wall outside, not a footprint this time, but a hand. Long fingers. Webbed slightly. Pressed flat against the siding just below the window, like something had stood there to watch him while he dreamed.

Except he wasn't sleeping anymore.

And the dreams still came.

Desperate to understand, he went back through the dive logs.

The fjord floor had changed.

That was the first thing that stood out, subtle shifts in depth readings, sonar shadows where none had been before. Something was rising.

Or something had moved.

He checked archival charts. Compared sediment patterns from two years ago, five, ten. There was a hollow now, a void where bedrock used to be. And above that hollow, a cluster of mineral interference that none of the models could explain.

A soft spiral. Barely perceptible.

Just enough to register when overlaid across multiple dive paths.

Just enough to mean something.

He dug out the old journal. Henrik Søreide. The fisherman from 1824.

The last five pages had been stuck together, Emil hadn't wanted to force them before. But now he peeled them apart carefully, one by one.

The final entries were shorter. Erratic.

"We should not have lifted it."

"It was not waiting to be found."

"It was dropped. As a seal. Not a gift."

"They do not rise unless called."

"We opened the gate with our hands."

There were no coordinates, no measurements. Just a sketch: a cairn on a ridge. A spiral carved into its side. A figure beside it, faceless, arms outstretched, something round held high overhead.

And beneath the drawing:

Seal the water. Seal the stone. Or forget your name forever.

Emil sat at the desk, hands trembling.

Outside, snow had begun to fall. Slow. Silent. As if the sky didn't want to interrupt the voices he could now hear just beneath the walls.

They weren't speaking yet.

They were listening.

The sonar image wasn't supposed to show anything new.

It was an automated sweep, uploaded by the research vessel *Skadi* a week before Anja's disappearance. A courtesy file. Standard bathymetric scan of Lysefjord's eastern shelf, shallow depths, nothing but sediment.

That's what he expected.

But the rendering blinked when he opened it.

A single black mass sat near the bottom of the image.

Circular.

Not massive, but not small either, maybe ten meters wide, subtle enough to miss if you weren't looking. Emil narrowed the contrast, overlaid the last three years of scans.

The shape hadn't been there before.

And it wasn't static.

There were faint distortions around it. Pressure blooms. Echo reverb not typical of stone or biological mass. The software suggested "silt drift." But silt didn't cast symmetrical shadows.

And it pulsed. Just faintly. Like a breath.

He stared at the screen, hand clamped around his mouth.

In the next frame, captured less than twenty seconds later, the shape had rotated slightly.

And the spiral was visible.

Etched into the sea floor.

As if something *beneath it* had pressed up and imprinted the shape outward, like a fingerprint rising from the palm of the earth.

He didn't move for a long time.

Didn't blink.

The wind outside picked up, a low constant groan, not quite whistling, more like pressure moving sideways.

The lights flickered.

He shut the laptop. Locked it in the drawer.

Then he sat down on the floor. The room had no temperature anymore, not cold, not warm, just **absent**, like heat and chill had both given up trying to define the space.

He rested his back against the wall, legs loosely folded, hands limp on his knees. The lights above him buzzed softly, not from power but from memory, as if the room still remembered what electricity used to sound like.

The spiral behind his ear pulsed once. Then again.

He closed his eyes.

The silence inside the station wasn't still. It **shifted**. The walls didn't creak, but they felt thinner. As though something on the other side was pressing gently, testing the separation.

He didn't speak. Didn't move.

Even breathing felt like a decision.

That night, the voices began again.

Not outside.

Inside.

Inside the walls, the floor, his skull. No language. Just tone. A deep, rhythmic chant, not sung but sustained, like the vibration of a choir buried beneath the fjord. The air in the station vibrated faintly. The spiral behind his ear throbbed in time with the hum.

He stood up, stumbled to the freezer, pulled the stone out of the bag.

Its spiral was fully open now.

The shape complete.

At the centre: a small divot, newly formed, no larger than the nail of his thumb.

Inside it, a single droplet of seawater, suspended. Unmoving. Never falling.

He blinked. Just once.

The droplet that had been clinging to the surface of the stone was gone. Vanished as though it had never existed at all. He blinked again, slower this time, uncertain whether he'd imagined it.

And now the spiral was gone too.

The carved groove, the mark that had haunted every waking hour, had vanished. In its place was only smooth stone, blank, pale, silent.

As if whatever the spiral had been meant to do had been done.

It had finished.

At 3:42 a.m., he heard a voice outside the window. Clear. Familiar. Anja's voice.

It wasn't a scream. Not a cry for help. Just his name, soft, uninflected, as if she were calling him from the hallway, asking a question she already knew the answer to.

"Emil?"

He didn't move.

A pause. Then again:

"I'm cold. Let me in."

His hand reached for the lamp, and he turned it off in a single motion. The room fell into darkness so suddenly it felt like the walls had folded in with it. He moved through the shadows toward the window, slowly, his footsteps muffled by the silence, by the stillness.

Outside, the snow had stopped falling.

The sky was moon-washed and empty, and the dock below glowed faintly in a shaft of pale light that landed like a spotlight across the wood.

She stood at the edge of it.

Barefoot. Coatless. Soaked.

Her skin glistened faintly in the cold, pale and slack, as if the blood beneath it had forgotten how to flow. She wasn't bloated. She wasn't rotted. But something about her was fundamentally **wrong**.

Her face hung in an expression that didn't match the moment. Her arms drooped too long at her sides, hands slack, unmoving. Her eyes were wide. Too wide. Not in fear, but in vacancy. Like someone had pried them open and left them there, like glass pressed too tightly into a frame. She didn't blink. She didn't shift her weight. She didn't breathe the way a person should when standing barefoot in that kind of cold.

She just waited.

He stepped closer to the glass, drawn by something beyond control, beyond reason.

Her lips moved.

"You called it. You showed it the way."

"Now it remembers."

Behind her, the water stirred.

Something rose, a shape, tall and thin, wrong in every proportion. It moved just beneath the surface, limbs impossibly long, dragging like ropes or tendons or bones pulled loose from structure. It didn't break the surface. It didn't splash. The water didn't react.

But it was there.

And it was staring.

Not at her.

At him.

Then she smiled.

Not with her mouth. That stayed slack, half-open, lips pale and still.

She smiled with her eyes. A flicker of intention, of knowledge, of something old now looking **through** her.

He stepped back from the window, breath caught in his throat, and with one swift motion, he pulled the blackout curtain shut, severing the view and burying the station in the dark.

When he turned, the mirror on the opposite wall was fogged.

Words had formed on the glass.

Drawn with a fingertip.

"SHE'S JUST THE FIRST."

"THE OTHERS KNOW YOU."

"THE OTHERS REMEMBER."

He turned on the tap, hands shaking slightly as he leaned over the sink. The water sputtered at first, then ran steady, cold and clear, or at least it appeared to be. He cupped a handful and splashed it across his face, hoping the shock would jolt something loose from the back of his skull, clear whatever was tightening behind his eyes.

But the water smelled faintly metallic.

Not like rust. Like blood.

He tasted salt on his lips before he realised he'd licked them. A brackish tang that didn't belong to the pipes, or the land, or any water meant for drinking.

He spat into the basin and shut the tap off.

But the drain kept gurgling.

At first, it sounded ordinary, residual suction, a pressure shift in the old pipes. He waited for it to fade.

It didn't.

The sound continued, long after the water had stopped, long after he'd stepped back from the sink, the faucet bone-dry.

The drain continued to pull. Not with force, but with intent. Like it wasn't draining anything, just *calling.*

Then came the sound.

It wasn't mechanical. Not the rattle of loose bolts or the deep groan of winter-strained plumbing.

It was a hum.

Low and sustained, rising from the metal like breath held too long.

Then that breath became real.

A slow inhale. Thick. Wet. Unmistakably close.

Then, from deep inside the pipe, closer than it should have been possible to sound. Came a voice:

"Let us out."

The Depth

He didn't tell anyone he was diving.

There was no one left to tell.

The last message he'd sent to the Oslo institute hadn't gone through, just a looping "unable to deliver" tag. The signal had been dropping for days, but this time it felt deliberate. ***Like the fjord was closing in behind him.***

So he planned the descent alone.

He hadn't used the dry suit in weeks. It smelled of dust and damp rubber when he unzipped the locker, but it held. The tanks were still good. He ran the compressor for half an hour just to be sure, but the hum it made wasn't right, too deep, too smooth. It sounded like the same tone he heard at night, bleeding through the walls when everything else went still.

He prepped the gear anyway. Not because he wanted to.

Because he had to.

Because the stone wasn't answering anymore. The surface had gone blank. The whisper had fallen silent. And Emil knew, the signal wasn't gone.

It had ***moved***.

Down.

The sky was slate grey by the time he launched the skiff. The fjord was calm. Flat enough to slice. A few birds circled overhead, but none landed. They hadn't for days. The further he moved from shore, the colder the air became. It sank into his bones, bypassing clothing, like the temperature itself was looking for a way inside him.

He reached the coordinates just past noon. Middle of the fjord. A hollow in the water where light seemed to fade faster. The sonar had marked it two days before, the imprint on the sea floor. Spiral shaped. Growing.

He checked his gear again. Mouthpiece. Gauge. Tank pressure.

Then dropped anchor.

He sat at the edge of the skiff, legs swinging over the side, and stared into the black beneath him.

There was no wind.

No sound.

Just the creak of the rope as it pulled taut, and the rhythmic knock of water against the hull.

Go now, a voice in his head said. It wasn't his voice, but it used his tone. His cadence.

He sat at the edge of the skiff, legs swinging over the side, and stared into the black beneath him.

There was no wind.

No sound.

Just the creak of the rope as it pulled taut, and the rhythmic knock of water against the hull.

Go now.

The voice echoed in his head, not his own, but close. Too close. It borrowed his cadence, his rhythm, his inner tone. Like someone wearing his thoughts from the inside out.

He leaned forward, both hands braced on the edge of the skiff. The water below was flat, black, expectant. His breath moved evenly through his mask, slow and focused, but somewhere beneath that calm, something waited. Not fear. Not resolve. Something older.

And then. Not by choice, not by intention, he whispered aloud:

"Every way leads deeper."

The words didn't belong to the moment. They didn't rise from memory. They arrived fully formed, calm and certain, as though spoken before or about to be spoken again. A loop, not a line.

He didn't hesitate.

He slipped into the water.

The cold struck him instantly, not like weather, but like punishment. Even through the thick insulation of the dry suit, it found seams and weak points, bit into skin, and sent nerves flaring in bursts of white across his back and shoulders. He exhaled hard, once, then steadied. Let his body adjust. Let the pressure build against him evenly.

He allowed himself to sink slowly, measured and quiet, tracking the descent as the world above dimmed. The surface folded over him without a sound.

Visibility fell off fast.

At ten meters, the water turned to smoke. At twenty, it was shadow. Thick, formless, the dark layered in movement and drift. The beam from his headlamp barely cut through, casting a narrow tunnel of clarity ahead. Suspended particles floated in front of his mask like ash in slow motion, not swirling, just *falling*, slowly, like everything else.

And then he saw it.

Below him. Faint at first.

A shape, darker than the dark around it. Still. Waiting. Growing.

At thirty meters, it revealed itself.

A stone.

Massive.

At least two meters across. Round. Partially buried in silt. Carvings visible even from above, a triple spiral this time, wider and deeper than the smaller objects. It didn't look placed. It looked *grown*. The rock around its edge had shifted, almost softened. Like it had fused with the seabed over time.

And at its centre, carved into the dark mass of stone with impossible symmetry, there was a hollow, deeper than the others, wide and smooth like something had been slowly worn down not by time, but by ritual.

Something pulsed faintly inside it.

Not light. Not energy.

Movement.

A soft, inward draw, steady and rhythmic, not mechanical, not even biological, but unmistakably alive. It pulled rather than radiated. Like breath taken not through lungs, but through stone. Through memory.

Emil hovered just above it, the thud of his heartbeat loud in his ears, thudding in time with something that wasn't his own.

Then, something shifted behind him.

A flicker. A change in current. Just enough to register.

He turned slowly, muscles dragging against the water, every movement cautious, controlled. There was nothing in sight, just particulate haze and blackness pressed flat against his headlamp's reach.

Still, something had moved.

He adjusted his position, let his body sink lower, descending gently toward the edge of the spiral. His headlamp cast its narrow cone across the sea floor, sweeping shadows across stone.

Then he saw it.

Off to the side. Just behind the main formation.

A shape.

Vertical. Still.

Human.

But not.

It stood upright on the seabed, unmoving, impossibly tall, its proportions distorted by both the water and by design. Its limbs were too long. Its torso narrow and straight. The skin or what passed for it. Was grey and seamless, sleek like seal hide, but too taut, too smooth.

Its arms hung at its sides, and its eyes were closed.

There was no tank. No breathing apparatus. No weight belt. No trail of bubbles.

Just presence.

And it was facing him.

Or rather, **aware** of him, watching without the need to open its eyes. That was the worst part. The certainty that it didn't need to *see* him to register him completely.

He wanted to surface.

Every instinct screamed it, memory, reflex, ancestral terror all pulling the same direction.

But his limbs wouldn't move.

His arms stayed locked in place, the rope in his grip going slack. His hands trembled, but the signal to *act* never made it past his spine.

Then the figure opened its eyes.

Black. Entirely. Not dark. **Depthless.**

No iris. No sclera. Just pressure, full and ancient and crushing. Like looking into something that remembered him before he was born.

And then the water began to shake.

Not with current. Not with movement.

With sound.

Low and full, a pressure wave that didn't travel through his ears but through his **bones**, his organs, his skull. It wasn't noise. It wasn't vibration.

It was a message.

Untranslated but absolute, something unspoken and vast that filled his chest like breath he hadn't taken. It expanded in his lungs, in his spine, in his teeth, as if the water itself had become aware of him from within.

His ears popped.

Then they burned.

The oxygen gauge on his wrist shuddered. The needle dipped violently, then bounced back as if it had been corrected by something watching the readout. His breath came in short, shallow draws, sharp and metallic now, like inhaling battery acid. Bubbles began to form around the inside of his mask.

Not air.

Boiling.

The oxygen in his system was **boiling.**

He kicked upward once, the motion sluggish, as if the water had thickened.

Then again, harder.

His foot caught the edge of the stone and for the briefest moment, the spiral lit with a soft, unnatural blue, glowing like a memory triggered.

And the figure turned.

Not with its body.

With its attention.

It shifted **into him,** like a spotlight narrowing, and for the first time, Emil knew what it meant to be *chosen*.

The ocean wasn't holding him down anymore.

It was pulling.

His mask cracked first, a soft, hairline fracture along the bottom edge, invisible until it wasn't. The pressure didn't spike the way it should have. It didn't surge. It **settled**, folding around him like fingers closing over a glass.

Then everything went bright.

Not from the surface, from below.

A soft blue radiance bloomed in his peripheral vision, slow and deliberate, like bioluminescence bleeding through bone.

He turned toward it, but the water dragged his limbs slower than thought. It wasn't resistance, it was delay, like moving through a dream.

The spiral in the stone glowed now.

Not fully. Just enough to show its lines were still wet. Still alive.

The humanoid figure stood before it, inches above the seafloor.

It hadn't risen.

It had waited.

It had remained there, eyes locked on him with a stillness that wasn't passive, but purposeful. Unblinking. Unreadable. And yet Emil knew. Not through logic or memory, but in that slow, icy way the body understands gravity. The figure recognised him. Not as an intruder. Not even as a visitor.

As a continuation.

Whatever had been summoned, whatever had noticed him in the

depths, hadn't discovered something new. It had remembered something lost. The transition wasn't clear. One moment, the ocean had been inside him, pressing, searing, unmaking. Pressure crushed in from all directions, his vision narrowing to a tight, collapsing tunnel, lungs drawing heat instead of air. Then, without memory of the ascent, without effort or action, he was back above the surface.

Cold air met his face like a slap.

He was sprawled across the deck of the skiff, gear tangled around his legs, mask skewed, coughing salt and blood onto the splintered wood. The breath he dragged in tasted old, like something dredged up from a flooded basement rather than gifted by the sky. His mouth burned. His hands shook.

He slumped back against the side of the skiff, lungs raw, throat hollow. The wind didn't touch him. The water no longer rocked beneath the boat. The whole fjord felt suspended. As if time itself had thinned to a single fragile thread.

He closed his eyes for what felt like a blink.

But when he opened them, he was no longer on the boat.

He was standing in a hallway.

Wooden. Narrow. Damp.

The walls wept moisture, planks swollen and darkened, warped from age or pressure. There were no doors. No light source. Just a dull, grey glow ahead, diffuse, source less, pulsing slightly in rhythm with the spiral behind his ribs.

He walked forward; feet bare against slick wood. Every step echoed too long, as though the hall extended far beyond its size. The sound of his breath was slow, deep, but not his own. He wasn't breathing. Something else was, and the air shifted with it.

Ahead, the hallway widened into a circular chamber.

On the far wall: a window.

Round. Thick glass. Looking out into black water.

Behind the glass, pressed close but not touching, stood a figure.

Tall. Still. Waiting.

Its eyes were open. Not accusing. Not pleading.

Just aware.

And Emil understood, with cold, perfect certainty, that it wasn't locked behind the window.

He was.

Above him, the sky offered no reprieve. A a smooth, grey lid stretched across the horizon, flat and motionless, not cloud so much as absence. No sun. No wind. Just the dead calm of something finished.

His dive computer blinked erratically on his wrist, depth readings corrupted, timestamps scattered or missing entirely. The tank gauge blinked red: zero.

He should have drowned.

His suit was torn, not at the joints or seams, but across his back. Wide, clean rips as if something had grasped and pulled. There was no sharp pain, but red had begun to seep through the inner lining, faint and persistent, radiating outward from a single point just below his shoulder blade.

He reached back, hand trembling, fingers brushing skin that should have been smooth.

It wasn't.

A raised ridge spiralled beneath his fingertips, precise, deliberate, warm. Not surface-warm. Not ambient. Warm from within.

He froze.

The shape wasn't scab or wound. It was carved. Not with a blade, but by something older and more exacting. The spiral matched what he had seen. What he had touched.

Now it was in him.

He leaned hard over the edge of the skiff and vomited. Not once, but in long, retching bursts, until there was nothing left to bring up. The taste that lingered wasn't seawater.

It was deeper.

Older.

Something elemental, like the copper sting of blood in the gums or the taste of ice that had never known sunlight.

He dropped the tank. Peeled off the dry suit. His limbs shook in waves, not from cold, from *misalignment*, like his joints had forgotten what it meant to be on land.

He caught his reflection in the porthole glass.

He looked thinner. Eyes darker. Skin sallow, stretched tighter across his skull. But it wasn't just the fatigue.

Something had gone missing in the deep.

And something else had come back in its place.

The lights in the corridor flickered as he stepped inside, not in warning, but in recognition. Like the system was adjusting to a presence it didn't fully trust. The air smelled wrong. It was faint, almost imperceptible, but enough: a mix of brine and metal and old stone. The scent you find in a place long buried. The kind that shouldn't follow you back from open water.

He paused by the sink, not to clean up, just to look at himself. The mirror above it was fogged, but not from steam. It refused to clear. He wiped at it once. The moisture returned instantly, as though his reflection didn't want to be seen.

Still, he could make out the shape of his own eyes.

Too dark.

Too wide.

Like something inside was watching back through them.

He pulled his collar higher around his neck, instinct more than modesty, trying not to touch the place where the spiral now lived. His skin there still radiated a soft, inward heat. Not burning. Not inflamed. But active. Like something waiting.

The station around him felt quieter than before. Not empty, just hushed, like a room holding its breath.

He didn't speak. Didn't announce his return. Just moved.

Quiet.

Careful.

And when he reached the lab, the lights above the desk didn't turn on until he sat down, not with the switch, but with presence alone.

He sat at the desk, still dripping, boots trailing moisture across the floor, and opened his laptop with fingers that barely felt like his own.

The dive log should have been empty. The pressure alone should have corrupted the data, or the sudden failure of power should have wiped the device entirely.

But there was a file waiting.

Audio only.

It sat at the top of the folder, timestamped but with no metadata, no location tag. Just a title.

WITNESS_01

He hesitated for a moment, then clicked it.

His voice played.

Not the words he'd spoken. Not in any language he knew. But the voice itself, the rhythm, the breath pattern, the familiar pauses between phrases. It was undeniably his.

The language, though, was wrong.

The sounds were sharp at the beginning of each utterance, then drawn out, as if the vowels had been stretched too far. Some ended in a rasp, others faded with a wet, guttural drag. It didn't sound like speech. It sounded like something mimicking it. The syllables clung to each other like teeth biting through cloth.

And yet it wasn't garbled. It wasn't distorted by water or interference.

It didn't sound like a recording at all.

It sounded like a transmission.

A broadcast, clear and deliberate.

He played it again.

The second time, there was more. A second layer crept in beneath the surface of the voice. A low harmony, quiet but present, rising just behind the first. It wasn't delay. It wasn't digital artefact. It was another voice, entering a fraction too late, speaking the same not-language a breath behind him.

Not echo.

Not repetition.

Chorus.

He stopped the playback.

His eyes dropped to his hands.

They looked wrong.

Paler than they should have been, the skin drawn tight across his knuckles. The shape was familiar, but the tone of it. The way they rested, the way they trembled slightly even now, made him feel like he was borrowing them.

And on his left palm, where there had been nothing when he surfaced, a faint spiral had begun to emerge.

It wasn't raised, not yet. But it was deeper than skin tone. The beginnings of something being written from the inside out.

Each breath he took now felt too full, like the air was saturated with water. Not damp. Submerged.

Every sound around him began from within. It was like he heard the room through his spine, not his ears.

He stood, slowly, and walked to the mirror above the sink, the real mirror. The one that hadn't fogged in over a week, even when the station lost power.

It was already misted.

Not evenly but smeared at the top right corner where a hand had touched the glass.

The print was large. The fingers too long. Webbed slightly at the tips.

It wasn't his.

And it was still wet.

He wiped the mirror clean with the sleeve of his shirt. The glass resisted for a moment, then cleared.

His reflection stared back.

No delay. No flicker. No trace of that subtle wrongness he had begun to expect.

Just him.

But something in his posture, in the exact tilt of the head and the hollowness around the eyes, felt observed rather than lived.

He raised one hand, slowly, deliberately, and pressed it to the centre of his chest. His fingers slid under the collar of his shirt, searching for confirmation he already feared.

And found it.

The stone.

Smooth, flat, unnaturally warm. It rested against his skin, embedded like something that had always belonged there. It didn't protrude. It didn't bruise. It had simply settled into place, as though he had grown around it.

He couldn't remember putting it in his pocket.

He couldn't recall ever lifting it from the dive tray or bringing it back at all.

But it was with him now.

And it was warm.

The Ship Returns

The fog came back just after nightfall.

It didn't roll in like it had before, slow, creeping, ghostlike. This time it arrived all at once, as if the air itself had thickened. One minute Emil could see the shoreline, the waterline, the tops of the ridges. The next, everything vanished.

The station might as well have been buried in ash.

He tried the floodlight outside. Nothing. The bulb flickered, popped, and went dark. He didn't bother with the generator. He knew it wouldn't start.

He stood in the window instead, forehead resting against the cold glass, breath fogging a small half-moon around his eyes.

The fjord was silent.

Even the birds had gone.

Then he saw it.

At first, just a shadow through the fog, tall and dark, hovering just offshore. He blinked. Waited. It didn't move.

No outline.

No wake.

It wasn't drifting anymore.

The shape sat low in the water, heavy, unmoving. Not pulled by current or tide. Anchored now. Fixed in place like something that had decided, finally, to arrive.

And it was closer than it had ever been before.

From the window, Emil could make out the details with unblinking clarity, the broken lines of the hull, curved and jagged where the wood had split. The planks were blackened, weather-rotted in places, their grain thick with salt and decay. Barnacles clung to the seams like parasites, fused into the joints, stubborn and ancient. The ship looked older than the sea that held it.

The dødningskipet.

Not just a whisper this time. Not just a shadow on the water or a story carried by wind.

It was here.

It was real.

And it had come to port.

Emil moved slowly to the front door, each step soft, measured, the weight of the moment pressing in from every direction. He didn't open it. His hand hovered just above the handle; breath caught in his chest.

Instead, he listened.

The silence was unnatural.

There was no wind now. No groan from the rafters or sway from the siding. The station stood as if held in place, like the building itself was waiting for instruction.

Then came the sound.

Not at the door.

At the windows.

A soft knock. Not sharp, not hurried. The kind of knock that didn't need to ask permission. Just present. Just enough to say we are here.

Then another, from a different pane.

Not repeated. Not mirrored.

Each knock had its own rhythm, its own pace. As if more than one hand now reached across the glass.

As if the house was being surrounded, not by bodies, but by intentions.

Like testing the structure. Or the distance between walls.

He crept to the bunk room. Pulled the curtain an inch aside.

A face blinked back at him from the other side of the glass.

Mottled skin. Hair flattened. Lips grey and swollen. But the eyes, wide, dry, too bright in the dark, were *alive*.

The figure in the window didn't blink.

It simply watched.

One hand pressed slowly to the glass, long fingered, webbed faintly at the joints, as if testing the barrier between worlds. The contact was silent, deliberate. No fog. No smudge. Just connection.

Emil stumbled backwards, feet unsure beneath him, hands catching the edge of the doorframe.

Then came the whisper.

It didn't enter the room from outside. It didn't slide through the walls or rise from behind.

It arrived inside him.

Not just inside his ears, deeper than that.

The voice curled into the folds of his brain, soft and intimate, spoken as though someone had leaned in close to his skull and breathed directly into thought.

"Emil."

Only that.

One word. His name.

The sound was quiet, almost gentle. Not threatening.

Just close.

He slapped both hands over his ears, trying to block it out, trying to shut down whatever breach had opened.

It didn't help.

The voice persisted.

"You've seen. You've heard."

Another pause. The words arrived slowly, spaced like they had waited years to be spoken aloud.

"Now remember."

A sharp pulse hit behind his eyes. His ears rang with the pressure, a frequency that wasn't quite sound but refused to be ignored.

He dropped to his knees.

The spiral on his palm began to itch, then flare with heat. A fire that didn't burn from above the skin, but from underneath. Rooted, rising.

He opened his hand.

The lines had changed overnight.

Where there had once been faint ridges, there were now black cracks etched deep into the skin, splitting like dried riverbeds across flesh. The pattern wasn't just cut into him. It was growing. Burrowing from within.

He crawled to the mirror, his breath catching in his throat.

His reflection stared back.

It didn't mimic him.

It didn't tilt its head or flinch or blink.

It just watched.

Then, without movement, without a change in expression, it whispered the same words again.

"Now remember."

His lips hadn't moved.

The sound had not come from the glass.

But the voice echoed through the room, impossibly clear, impossibly inside.

The whispering didn't stop.

It wove through the walls, through his pulse, through the spiral at the centre of everything.

Even when he moved away from the mirror, even after he shut the lights off, it followed him through the walls. Through the pipes. Through his own body. Not loud. Never loud.

Just *constant.*

The station was colder now. Not from the weather. Not from power loss.

From the ship.

It was still out there.

He could feel it, like a stone in the lung of the fjord, too heavy to float, too old to sink. Anchored not by rope but memory. It didn't need motion. It *was* motion. Or the end of it.

Emil stumbled to the kitchen, fingers numb, boots leaving wet prints across the floor. The windows were completely fogged now. Salt crusted along the edges of the glass, weeping down in thin threads like veins.

He grabbed the emergency tarp and hammer from the utility cabinet. Began covering the windows, one by one. Not because he thought it would keep anything out, but because he couldn't stand seeing them anymore.

The watchers were closer now.

No longer shapes at a distance or silhouettes at the edge of the dock. They stood directly at the windows, their forms pressed close to the glass. Their faces were visible in the low light, not expressionless, but composed. Patient. As if they had been here before. As if they had stood in this exact position, watching through this very window, a hundred times or more.

And each time, someone else had been on the other side of the glass.

Someone waiting. Someone not yet ready.

Emil's breath was short as he hammered faster at the tarp, fists tight, adrenaline rising with each pulse in his neck. The thick fabric snapped once in the wind, and in the same instant, something knocked back.

Not a thud. Not a slam.

Just three soft, deliberate knocks.

Right beneath his hand.

Measured.

He froze, hand still pressed against the pane, heart pounding too loud in the quiet room.

A moment later, the same rhythm came again, not from the same window, but from the next one over. The sound was identical. The timing exact. Then a third set of knocks, from somewhere on the back wall. All spaced perfectly. Calm. Coordinated.

They weren't asking to come in.

They didn't need to.

He was already surrounded.

He backed into the hallway, chest tight, ears ringing. The whisper had become more organised now — not just repetition, but *conversation*. Not in any language he knew, but *structured*, like call and response.

Two voices.

One just ahead of him.

One just behind.

"He hears."

"He remembers."

"He accepts."

Emil fell against the wall, breath hitching.

He stumbled to the back of the station, to the lab, to the one room where he thought the air might still belong to him. The freezer sat in the corner, lid sealed tight.

He approached it slowly.

The lock had been snapped.

The spiral stone was gone.

But something had been left in its place.

A line of seaweed, long, braided, coiled like a rope. Still wet. Still dripping. At first he thought it was just a trail of algae, but then it twitched.

Moved.

And began to unwind itself across the floor, sliding like it had purpose.

He stepped back too quickly, foot catching on the cord to the backup light.

The battery sparked.

A sharp crack lit the corner of the room, followed immediately by the sound of glass giving way. The bulb above him shattered with a sudden pop, fragments scattering across the floor like frost breaking underfoot.

Then everything went black.

No flicker. No warning.

Just gone.

From outside, a noise followed, not loud, but heavy. The groan of wood against wood, like a beam shifting under strain or a hull brushing something too close. Then came a deeper sound, low and slow, as if something massive was settling itself into place, not with urgency but finality.

Emil moved without thinking.

He ran to the front window and tore the tarp aside, pulling it back just enough to peer through the glass.

The ship was there.

Fully docked now, sitting heavy in the water with a presence that felt older than the tide. There was no wake trailing behind it, no anchor chain glinting in the moonlight, no sign of approach.

It had not arrived.

It had appeared.

A thick rope stretched from the side of the hull to the cleat at the end of the pier. It looked like it had been woven from seaweed and tendon, organic and wet, pulsing faintly as it held tension.

Something hung from it.

A shape. A weight. A bundle, swaying gently in the air.

Emil leaned closer, squinting against the fogged glass.

It was a body.

Anja.

Or something that had once worn her shape.

Her limbs moved too slowly, drifting with a softness that defied gravity. Not suspended in air. Suspended in something else — denser, invisible. Her arms floated up and curled slightly at the elbows. Her feet didn't dangle. They hovered.

Her head turned with fluid precision.

And her eyes found his.

She smiled.

It was small. Closed-lipped. Familiar.

Then her mouth moved, slow and deliberate, shaping words that made no sound.

Come back.

Inside his ears, the whisper pulsed again. It matched the rhythm of the ship, a thudding cadence that beat through his chest — not as emotion, but as signal. It was a heartbeat, but not one he recognised. Not his. Not hers.

Not human.

Then the station began to respond.

The walls exhaled. Not with sound, but with pressure. And the seams, not cracks, not fractures, but clean architectural joins, began to bleed. Thin black water beaded along every edge. Window frames. Door seams. Even between the floorboards. It didn't surge. It didn't pour.

It moved toward him.

Not quickly.

But with certainty.

He stumbled backwards into the bunkroom, slipping on the wet boards, boots striking hard against the floor. Panic flickered at the edge of reason, and he scrambled for the only thing that still felt like it might hold meaning: his journal.

When he opened it, the last page was already filled.

Typed.

Not by his hand.

Two lines only.

The gate has opened.

The witness has spoken.

The lights flickered once behind him, a single pulse that didn't return.

The floor groaned beneath him, not from his own weight, but from something moving beneath the structure, shifting the bones of the station.

Then came the sound he had feared most.

Boots on the dock.

Heavy. Measured. Not rushing.

Not his.

Not hers.

Another noise followed, deeper and closer — the soft, strained creak of a ship adjusting to new weight.

Emil didn't need to look.

He knew.

They were disembarking.

Not to knock.

But to collect.

Unsealing

He didn't remember retrieving the stone.

One moment, Emil had backed into the far corner of the lab, the sea leak pressing at the walls, voices speaking directly behind his eyes.

The next: it was in his hand.

No bag. No gloves.

Just the stone, heavier now, dense with a wrongness that felt physical. The spiral was no longer shallow. It had deepened into a hollow groove, like something had turned inside it.

The centre glowed faintly.

It wasn't glowing. Not brightly.

Just awake.

The stone pulsed softly in his hand, its surface warm now, not hot, not threatening, but undeniably alive. Emil dropped it onto the floor, letting it fall hard against the concrete. The impact rang sharp, echoing off the steel leg of the bench beside him.

But it didn't crack.

He stared at it, then picked it up again, hands trembling, and hurled it with force against the far wall.

It bounced once, struck the floor, clattered across the tiles, and rolled to a stop.

Still whole.

Still pulsing.

It hadn't even chipped.

His breath caught as frustration built in his chest, sharp and breathless. He crossed to the tool shelf and grabbed the heavy iron mallet, the one used for driving anchor spikes and mooring pins. The weight of it grounded him briefly, something real, something built for force. He raised it high above the stone.

That was when the voice came.

"Don't."

It wasn't loud. Just there. He turned sharply, eyes darting to the doorway. Empty.

No one.

But the stone had warmed again, a little stronger now, as if responding to his hesitation. He held the mallet steady.

"Don't."

This time, it came from the stone itself, not through the air, but inside it. Inside him. He brought the hammer down with a shout, all strength, all desperation, and struck.

The blow landed hard.

But the sound it made wasn't what he expected. It didn't crack like rock. It rang out sharp and wet, like hitting bone. The mallet recoiled from the impact and flew from his hand, clattering across the floor.

Pain shot up his arm.

He looked down and saw that his palm had split cleanly at the centre, a fast, thin arc tearing through the skin. It wasn't swollen. There was no bruise. Just blood, vivid and hot, spilling from the wound as though something inside had forced its way out.

The spiral that had been carved into him now looked mirrored, not only beneath his skin, but across the stone itself.

He screamed, falling back. Clutched his hand as the pain surged, not like a burn or a cut, but like a command.

The stone didn't move.

It didn't crack.

It simply sat there.

Still whole.

Still breathing.

And as the blood dripped from Emil's hand onto its surface, it soaked into the spiral groove without resistance. It absorbed the red like ink pulled into parchment, ancient and waiting.

He wrapped the hand in gauze with quick, shaking fingers. Not because he believed it would help. It wouldn't. But it might slow the bleeding.

The pain didn't throb now.

It pulsed.

And it pulsed in time with the whispering that still threaded through his head, steady, soft, constant. On the desk behind him, the journal lay open.

The last page.

He had avoided it until now, too afraid of what might be waiting.

But now it called to him.

The ink was still drying, smudged faintly where his fingers had brushed the edge. The handwriting was his. Undeniably. The loop of the lowercase "e." The quick, slanted "t." The hurried scrawl of the "a" in his name. He hadn't written it.

But he had.

Final Entry

The gate is open.

The name has changed, but the role remains.

You are the new witness.

The spiral is now memory.

The ship waits for no second calling.

You saw it. That was enough.

E. Strand

The Second Remembering

He stood there for a long time, reading it again and again. The words didn't change. They didn't fade or blur. They simply stayed.

True.

Around him, the station began to groan softly. Not from wind.

From weight. He stepped slowly toward the door. His boots sank slightly into the floorboards, the wood had softened beneath him, waterlogged and damp, as if the sea had already begun to reclaim the station from below.

He opened the door.

Fog rolled in immediately. Thick and wet. Thicker than anything he'd seen before. It moved like smoke, not mist, and tasted of salt and silt.

But beyond it, the dock was clear.

And the ship was waiting.

Fully visible now, no longer half-hidden in fog or shadow. Its hull rose high above the pier, black and jagged and real. Light glowed from the portholes, soft and low, not electric, not fire. Something older.

Something remembered.

Figures moved along the deck. They didn't rush. They didn't speak. They didn't search. They were simply there.

Present.

A ramp had been extended from the ship's side and now rested perfectly against the end of the dock. It hadn't dropped or slid or been lowered.

It had arrived.

Welcoming.

Expectant.

And carved into the boards at Emil's feet, where the dock met the station, words waited for him. Not scratched. Not painted.

Carved.

> **You've seen it.**
> **You've heard it.**
> **Now walk.**

The dock groaned beneath his boots as Emil stepped out into the fog.

The cold hit him differently now, not sharp like before, not biting. It was *still*. Thick. Like walking through memory. Every breath he took carried weight, like air soaked in sleep. He could feel the spiral in his palm, pulsing faintly beneath the gauze, syncing with his steps.

The ramp extended from the ship in a gentle curve, almost elegant. Not crude wood like the rest of the hull. This part was newer. Or preserved. It bore no moss, no rot, no sea damage. It looked... *intact.*

Waiting.

He reached the edge of the dock.

Paused.

And looked back once at the station.

The windows glowed with faint gold — not light, but reflection. As if fire burned behind them, though he knew the power was dead.

He turned back to the ship.

Took his first step.

The wood beneath his boots shifted.

Not in a creak or sag of old construction, but with purpose, a slow, deliberate flex, as if the ramp itself had inhaled slightly beneath his weight. Like the ship was not a structure, but something alive. Something holding its breath.

He placed one foot in front of the other, moving slowly, carefully, each step heavier than the last. The sound of his tread echoed too sharply, louder than it should have been, as if the ramp had been built to carry the noise forward. Behind him, the fog closed in completely.

The dock disappeared into it without resistance. The station was gone.

He didn't look back. As he reached the top of the ramp, he stepped fully onto the deck.

And the ship did not move.

There was no sway, no shift beneath his feet. It held perfectly still. Not because it was anchored, not because of tide or balance, but because it chose to remain steady. No lines tethered it to the dock.

No chain secured it in place. It simply *was*.

The deck boards beneath him were dry.

Completely dry.

Smooth to the touch, as if they had never known water, despite the damp air and heavy fog surrounding the vessel. The moisture in the air clung to his clothes and skin, but not a drop lingered here.

The silence pressed in hard. No gulls cried overhead. No waves lapped against the hull. Not even the creak of rigging or the slap of wind against canvas. There was no movement at all.

Only whispering.

It had grown clearer now, closer, a constant thread of sound just beneath the skin of the moment. And for the first time since it began, it wasn't in his head anymore.

It came from the ship itself, the walls, the deck, the railing. Every plank held a voice. And they were all saying the same word: *"Witness."*

He turned slowly, every motion feeling weighted, as if the air itself had thickened around him.

Figures lined the deck now.

They stretched from one side of the vessel to the other, ten, twenty, maybe more. He didn't bother counting. There were too many. And something about the way they stood made the numbers irrelevant. Shoulder to shoulder, they formed a wall of silence, barefoot and unmoving, each with eyes wide open, not with surprise or fear, but with a kind of hollow certainty. They were still, but not lifeless.

They were drowned.

And every one of them bore the same mark.

Some had it carved into their chests, deep and deliberate. Others wore it seared into the palms of their hands, burned black into the flesh. A few carried it behind the curve of the ear, subtle and curling, like it had grown there instead of being placed. Wherever it appeared, the shape was always the same.

A spiral.

Their mouths remained closed.

But still, he could hear them whispering.

It wasn't loud. Not like voices rising from throats. It was softer, closer, like breath passed directly into bone. A susurration that threaded through the air like fog.

He stepped forward and began to walk between them.

Not one of them moved, but he felt their gaze track him as he passed, dozens of eyes shifting in unison, not hostile, not pleading. Just following.

He moved past the mast, tall and warped, its wood split along one side. A length of rope had been lashed around the fracture, the fibres frayed with age but pulled tight, as if they were holding the whole thing together. The rope didn't swing. Nothing did. Not even the bell mounted above the helm, though he heard it ringing faintly in his ears, a sound that shouldn't have existed but clung to the air like memory.

At the centre of the deck, the hatch was waiting.

Open.

The cover lay folded back on its hinges, and a steep wooden stairwell led down into darkness.

He hesitated only for a breath, then began to descend without speaking.

The air shifted as soon as he moved below deck.

Each step he took carried him deeper into a different kind of atmosphere. The temperature rose slightly, not enough to sweat, but enough to notice. The pressure increased, too, pushing gently against his chest and shoulders. The space felt close. Not narrow, heavy. As though the sea itself pressed against the hull from the outside, waiting patiently for an excuse to rush in. He had the sudden impression that even a single breath, taken too deeply or released too loudly, might invite the water to flood through the walls.

At the bottom of the stairs, a corridor stretched out in both directions.

To his left, a row of narrow bunks lined the wall. Hammocks hung loosely from rusted hooks, and though there was no breeze, they swayed just slightly, not enough to call attention to, but enough to suggest someone had left them only moments before.

To his right, a single door stood out.

Painted matte black, it absorbed the low light rather than reflecting it. The surface was scarred deeply in hundreds of places. The scratches overlapped, clustered, gouged into the wood at wild angles. It wasn't graffiti. It wasn't decoration.

It looked like panic.

As if hands had scraped and clawed, not just to open the door, but maybe to keep it closed. Or to get back through from the other side.

He reached out and opened it.

The hinges resisted slightly before giving way, and the door creaked just once as it swung open. Inside, the room was bare. A single chair stood at its centre, turned to face a mirror bolted directly to the far wall. The mirror had fogged slightly, a thin layer of condensation misting its surface. And there, drawn through the fog in a clean spiral, was the mark, sharp, deliberate, as though someone had traced it with a fingertip.

Below it, scratched into the glass with something pointed and sharp, a line of text waited:

WHAT YOU WITNESS, YOU BECOME.

He stepped closer, drawn in, unable to look away.

In the mirror, his reflection met him.

It was his face, but worn, hollow, the skin drawn tighter across the cheekbones, the colour dulled to a pale grey. Behind his left ear, the spiral had risen fully now, swollen like an old scar pushed to the surface. It throbbed faintly, in time with his breath.

But something else caught his eye.

In the mirror, just behind him, the corridor was no longer empty.

Figures moved in the reflection, dozens of them, far more than he had seen above deck. They filled the narrow hallway, spilled into the stairwell, pressed in shoulder to shoulder. Not rushing. Not hostile. Simply present.

He turned around instinctively.

Nothing.

The corridor behind him was silent. Still. Empty.

But when he turned back to the mirror, the figures had come closer.

They were almost behind him now; their eyes locked on his back.

He felt the memory surface before he understood what it meant.

A book.

A room.

A sealed box tucked into the back corner of a library in Edinburgh.

And a man named Bryce.

His eyes closed of their own accord as the voices returned, low and sure, threading through his thoughts like a current he had always known was there.

Yes.   *Now*   *you*   *remember.*

Now we begin.

The Offering

He waited until just before dawn.

Not for safety. Not for clarity.

But because something inside him knew the tide would be lowest then.

And something down there needed to see him clearly.

The skiff rocked lightly against the dock as he climbed in, the same small vessel he'd used on that first descent , before the ship returned, before the station cracked and sang and swallowed his voice. He didn't bring lights. He didn't bring tools. Just the oars, the spiral stone wrapped in canvas, and the weight in his chest.

He didn't bother locking the station behind him.

Nothing there left to protect.

Nothing left to *close*.

The fog had receded for the first time in days, retreating into the valleys like a breath held in too long. The sky was thin and grey, the water beneath it utterly still. No gulls. No wind.

Just silence.

And the slow lap of the oars as he rowed out into the centre of the fjord.

He turned slowly, every motion heavy with hesitation, as though the air around him had thickened.

The deck was no longer empty.

Figures now lined both sides, shoulder to shoulder, unmoving and barefoot, their feet planted as if rooted to the ship itself. Ten, then twenty, too many to count without stopping. They stood in complete silence, and though none of them spoke, every one of them watched.

Their eyes were wide, too wide. Not with fear. Not with wonder. But with knowing.

They were drowned, each of them. And each bore the same mark. Some had spirals burned into the palms of their hands. Others carried them seared across their chests or etched delicately behind the curve of one ear like an infection that had grown precise. The pattern repeated again and again, perfectly formed, no variation.

Their mouths were shut.

Yet the whispering had not stopped.

If anything, it had grown louder.

He walked between them, the deck silent underfoot. None of the figures moved as he passed, not even a shift of posture or breath.

But their eyes followed him.

Every single one.

He moved beyond the mast. A tall, cracked beam, its timber split and worn with age. One side had been lashed tightly with rope, the kind that looked too old to hold but refused to let go. The rope didn't sway in the mist. It simply hung. Above the helm, a bell swung ever so slightly, though there was no wind to carry it. It didn't ring.

But Emil could hear the echo of it anyway, faint and constant, like the memory of a sound still caught in the air.

He reached the centre of the deck.

A hatch stood open at his feet, its cover tilted back on rusted hinges, revealing a steep set of stairs that descended into shadow. He paused only briefly, then stepped down into the dark without a word.

The air changed almost immediately.

With each step, it grew warmer, thicker. The pressure pressed in against his shoulders and ribs, not suffocating, but certain. It felt as though the sea itself had crowded in around the hull, waiting just beyond the walls, held back by silence, by stillness. And if he exhaled too hard, it might find a way through.

At the bottom of the stairs, a narrow corridor stretched ahead.

To his left, a row of empty bunks lined the wall. Hammocks hung from rusted hooks, and though no movement stirred the space around them, they swayed gently, as if someone had left them moments before.

To the right, a single door broke the rhythm of the corridor.

Painted black.

Its surface was scratched in dozens of places. No, hundreds, As if hands had tried to claw their way in. Or out. The marks criss-crossed and tangled like an archive of panic etched into wood.

He reached for the handle and opened it.

Inside, the room was small.

A single chair faced a mirror bolted to the far wall. The mirror's glass was clouded with condensation, and in its centre, drawn with a fingertip, was the spiral, clean, deliberate, impossible to miss.

Beneath it, etched into the surface with something sharp, a line of text:

WHAT YOU WITNESS, YOU BECOME.

He stepped forward, eyes fixed to the reflection and stared.

His own face looked back at him. Hollow-cheeked. Grey-skinned. His eyes sunken deeper than he remembered. The spiral behind his ear had risen fully now, no longer a mark but a scar, thick and raised, curling like a brand just beneath the skin.

But he wasn't alone in the mirror.

Behind him, faint but clear in the glass, figures moved. More than he had seen above. They filled the corridor behind him, filled the stairwell, packed in shoulder to shoulder, watching just as the ones above had done.

He turned quickly.

Nothing.

The hallway was still.

Empty.

Silent.

But when he looked back into the mirror, the figures had moved closer.

He blinked. And suddenly, something surfaced in his mind — not memory exactly, but clarity. A detail pulled forward from the depths of his own thoughts.

A book.

A room.

A sealed box in a library in Edinburgh.

And a man named Bryce.

He closed his eyes as the whispering settled into a shape, into a voice, clear and calm, no longer distant.

"Yes. Now you remember."

"Now we begin."

But the voices didn't stop.

They swelled.

Risen now beyond vibration, beyond tone, a presence that filled the sky, pressed down on the fjord, and curled into the back of Emil's throat like smoke he hadn't inhaled.

He gripped the sides of the skiff. His knuckles were white. His breath refused to steady. It didn't feel like air anymore. It felt *borrowed*.

The water beneath the boat began to hum, a low, subsonic throb that passed up through the hull and into his bones.

The singing grew clearer.

It wasn't language.

But it was directed.

Not outward. Not to the sky.

To him.

The spiral burned on his palm again, as though the act of giving hadn't ended anything, only completed a circuit.

"You've done it," the voices seemed to say.

"Now we can finish the remembering."

He tried to speak. Tried to ask what they meant.

But no sound left his mouth.

Not because he was afraid.

Because his body wouldn't let him.

His voice was no longer his own.

The skiff shifted beneath him, not sharply, but with a slow, deliberate tilt to starboard. As though something immense beneath the surface had shifted its weight. Emil reached for the side, steadying himself against the motion, then leaned over to look.

The water still shimmered in the faint light, its surface deceptively calm. But now, beneath it, something moved. Not from the depths below, but from some impossible distance. It was rising not through space, but through time, drawn upward as though memory itself was breaching.

A shape emerged.

A ship.

Not the **Dødningskipet.** Not the rotted vessel that had been docked at the station, tethered to his reality by salt and myth. This one was older, untouched by decay, its lines smooth and unbroken, its hull whole. It passed just beneath the surface of the fjord, not disturbing the water, but reflecting through it with unnatural clarity, like a memory pressing into glass. Each detail aligned perfectly with its counterpart above: shadow for shadow, plank for plank, a ghost of the original.

An echo.

Etched into the prow was the spiral, not weathered, not worn, but fresh. As though it had been carved only moments ago. Or was about to be.

Figures lined the deck of the vessel, standing in still formation, shoulder to shoulder, silent and watching.

And then, one turned.

His face. His posture. His coat.

It was Emil.

But younger.

Unmarked.

Clean of the spiral, clean of the weight that now sat behind his eyes. This version of himself had not yet stood on a deck surrounded by the drowned. Had not yet heard the whispering. Had not yet been named.

This was the Emil from before. Before the fjord had remembered him. Before he had remembered the fjord. The reflection met his gaze with unsettling calm and smiled. Not widely. Not cruelly. Just a faint curl of recognition.

As if to say:

We've done this before.

We'll do it again.

The Mirror Ship

The ship passed directly through him, not physically, but with a pressure that filled his chest and pushed against his ribs from the inside out. It felt like time itself exhaling, a great lung releasing centuries of breath.

The skiff rocked gently once more.

And the world fell quiet.

He turned slowly in his seat, gaze sweeping the fog.

The station was gone.

The dock had vanished too, swallowed completely by the mist now curling low over the water's surface. There were no lights shining through it. No outline of walls. No door. No roof. Not even the shadow of watchers waiting within.

Only water.

Open and still.

Further back, where the *Dødningskipet* had rested for days, there was now nothing but mist.

It hadn't sailed.

It hadn't sunk.

It had simply withdrawn, leaving no trace, as if the moment had never happened, as if it had only been waiting for its role to be fulfilled.

Above him, the sky had begun to lighten.

Not with dawn. There was no gold on the horizon, no warmth rising through the air. This was a colder shift, a paler shade bleeding through the grey. It felt less like sunrise and more like the world resetting, clearing the stage now that the scene had played.

The offering had been accepted.

Or perhaps it had never been an offering at all.

Emil rowed in silence.

No voices followed.

The whispering that had filled his mind for days had gone quiet, not in retreat, but in completion. But the spiral on his palm pulsed steadily, each beat a reminder that what had begun was not over.

By the time the skiff reached the shore, the tide had come in. The beach was lined with footprints. Dozens of them. Pressed deep into the wet sand. They ran in both directions, parallel, unwavering.

Barefoot.

Too wide-spaced to be human.

Too straight to have wandered.

He stepped off the boat and onto the shore.

The wind shifted slightly, brushing against his coat, and it carried no salt, no chill.

Only a single word, carried softly through the rustle of trees and the damp hush of morning:

Witness.

Back at the station, the journal lay open.

The final page, which he had once seen as blank, now held a new paragraph, one that had not been there before.

The text was typed.

Not printed. Not handwritten. Typed, with keystrokes he hadn't heard from a machine that hadn't been turned on.

The spiral remains open. The remembering has only begun.
There was never an offering. Only permission. He remembers.
And now we begin again.

Below it, two initials:

E.S.

His own. He closed the journal with care, the edges damp from the air. Above the sink, the mirror had fogged. He stepped toward it, heart steady now.

No figure stood behind him this time.

Only the spiral.

Drawn clearly into the steam.

But now it had changed.

It was no longer a sign etched for others to find.

It was inverted.

Not opening out.

But folding in.

The Archivist

Oslo, five weeks later.

The city moved like it always had, slow, thoughtful, heavy with winter. A wet snow fell without urgency, the sky the colour of smudged glass.

Inside the National Historical Registry, tucked between the conservation wing and a locked annex no one talked about, a woman named **Liv Halvorsen** was halfway through cataloguing regional disappearance cases when the package arrived.

No postmark. No return address.

Just her name, typed on the label. Neat. Precise.

She didn't open it right away.

Not because she was scared, that would come later, but because it wasn't unusual. Researchers sent odd things all the time. Boxes of bones. Disks without explanation. Diaries, maps, unlabelled photographs. It was her job to sort them. To assign context. To decide what mattered.

But something about this one itched at the back of her neck.

She turned the box over in her hands. It had a smell, faintly organic. Like old wood soaked in brine. The paper was soft, almost velvety, and too cold for the room it had been sitting in.

She opened the package with care, hands moving slowly as if she already understood that what lay inside mattered, not just to someone, but to the shape of something larger.

Inside, resting neatly within the weather-stained wrapping, was a journal. The cover was leather, sun-cracked and salt-warped, the kind of material that had travelled. The edges were curled inwards like dried petals, browned and brittle, their softness worn away by years of damp and friction.

Tucked just inside the cover, folded with deliberate precision, was a photograph. She paused before touching it, then unfolded it carefully, letting the paper spread out in her palm.

It showed a stone.

Not the smooth, symmetrical artefact she'd seen in prior reports, not the "Subject A" spiral logged in earlier field files. This one was different. The carving at its centre was still a spiral, but the lines were interrupted, jagged in places. Smaller runes surrounded it, but their shapes were sharper, more aggressive. And the stone itself looked fractured, rough across its surface, chipped along the edges, as if it had been exhumed in a rush or uncovered by mistake. There was an unevenness to it. Something unfinished. Something forgotten twice over.

There was no accompanying note.

No letter.

No tag identifying where it had come from or why it had been sent. Just the journal.

And the photo.

She held the book in her hands for a moment, then turned to the final page with a kind of quiet dread. The handwriting was uneven, slanting across the page in a script that had clearly been written in haste. Parts of it had faded. Not with age, but with exposure. Salt had blurred several of the lines, and the ink in places had bled into the fibres.

But the name was still legible.

Emil Strand.

Her heart skipped slightly. She didn't need to check the database. She knew that name.

It had surfaced twice in her work over the past few years, once in a missing persons bulletin filed out of Lysefjord, flagged discreetly under an "at risk researcher" tag, and again in a more obscure Oslo listing. That one had come through unofficial channels, buried beneath layers of clearance, asking for high-level access to restricted marine logs from a closed expedition site.

The file had gone cold within a week.

No formal follow-up. No statements. No closure.

Just gone.

No media. No family push. No trace.

Like someone had decided he had already gone where he was meant to and no one was to follow. She flipped back a few pages. Scanned the contents. It didn't read like a personal journal.

It read like a **warning.**

Entries out of order. Some repeated. Some crossed out and rewritten in what looked like a different hand, the same words, but different rhythm.

Mentions of carved stones. Spirals. Voice hallucinations. Names she didn't recognise, **Henrik Søreide**, **Anja Kvamme**. Listed like footnotes in the margin.

Each followed by the word: **Witness.**

She placed the photo flat on the desk. Pulled the lamp closer. Examined the runes again. They didn't match anything in her archive. Not Norse. Not Sámi. But something in them felt deliberate. Like someone had copied symbols by memory, not meaning.

A tag had been paperclipped to the back.

Three words typed in red ink:

DO NOT OPEN.

She'd seen that tag before. Only twice.

Once in a file marked ***ARCHIVED / REDACTED ORDER — NORDIC (SAGAS).***

Once on a sealed envelope that had gone straight into deep storage.

It was a classification used only by internal archivists.

Liv's predecessor had called it a joke. "Just paranoia with paperwork," he'd said. "Old stories boxed up and filed by ghost hunters."

But the cataloguing number was real. She pulled up the system and typed in the redacted code.

The screen flashed once. Then opened a file with no author.

No summary.

Just a list of contents.

Line 14: *Recovered Object, Fjord Site 3b. Engraved stone, spiral motif. Classified Artifact. Do not translate.*

Line 15: *Subject: Emil Strand. Status: Witnessed.*

Line 16: *Secondary journal received. Contamination level pending.*

She looked down at the book again, letting her eyes move slowly across the pages. The salt had warped the paper, and in several places, the ink had run, forming soft halos around words that had once been sharp. Symbols bled faintly through from the reverse of the pages, spirals drawn into the margins, some barely visible, others bold and deliberate, layered as though they had been traced again and again.

One entry near the end caught her eye. It had no date. No entry number. No context.

Just words.

The spiral was not ours to unearth.
We were never meant to remember.
But we do. Now we do.
And so it begins again.

She read the lines twice, then closed the book gently, letting the weight of the cover press the pages flat. Without ceremony, she stood, crossed to the far drawer beneath the cabinet, and filed the journal by hand. It slid into place behind a locked panel, already marked for restricted access. She keyed in a temporary override.

Classification: REDACTED ORDER

Tag: Unconfirmed Contact, Fjord Series

Status: Pending Containment

The confirmation light blinked once, then dimmed.

She leaned back in her chair, hands resting in her lap, the weight of the book still lingering in her muscles.

And exhaled.

The breath came slowly, and with it, the faintest shift in the atmosphere, not colder exactly, but thinner. As if the room had been quietly altered. Not by force. Not by event.

Just changed.

Like something had left through a door she hadn't noticed.

Or something had entered and chosen not to announce itself.

Either way, the room had gone still.

Not peaceful.

Just… quiet.

Not the kind of quiet that comes from late hours or snowfall.

This was deeper. Full. The silence of held breath. Of water just before it breaks.

Liv sat back from the desk, eyes still on the file. The journal. The single phrase typed in red. ***DO NOT OPEN***. still pulsing behind her eyes like an afterimage. Her fingertips tingled where they'd touched the paper.

She rubbed them together.

The air still felt dry. Not arid, not stale. Just touched with something electric. A faint tingling at the edge of sensation, like static in the fingertips or the moment before a storm breaks. She pushed back from her desk, the chair rolling slightly as she rose. Her body moved out of habit more than intent, driven by the need to stretch, to move, to shake off the tension building beneath her skin.

That's when she saw it.

A shape. Faint, but present, just beneath the edge of the desk.

She leaned down slowly, brow furrowing, and ducked to get a closer look. The lighting was dim underneath, shadows pooling, but there it was.

A mark.

Not a smudge or scratch, something deliberate. She reached out, ran her fingers along the underside of the desk, letting her skin trace the shape in the wood.

It was real.

Not sketched hastily.

Not scrawled in pencil or ink.

Carved. Clean, precise, and old. The grooves were smooth at the edges, worn slightly by time, as though the desk had been hiding it for years.

It wasn't a mistake.

It was left.

Or worse, it had always been there, just waiting for someone to notice.

Rough but deliberate. A spiral. Exactly like the one in the photo. Small. Tucked just out of sight. Not symmetrical. Slightly elongated, like whoever had made it had rushed near the end.

She stood slowly.

Brows furrowed.

She hadn't carved it.

No one else used this desk. Her name had been on this office since her first day. Two years ago. She'd taken it over from the archivist before her, whose name she couldn't remember, no matter how many times she tried. She swore someone had said it aloud to her at the handoff, but it was *gone*. Just an impression now, like a label peeled off glass.

She eased herself back into the chair, the familiar creak of the frame grounding her just enough to take the next step. With a practiced motion, she opened her terminal, not to work, not to analyse, but simply to clear her thoughts, to focus her mind on something procedural.

The login screen blinked. A flicker, nothing major. Then the system caught up, and her credentials loaded.

The cursor sat in the centre of an empty note field, blinking steadily.

Then, before she could touch the keyboard, letters began to appear, slow, measured, one by one, as if each had been chosen deliberately:

A R C H I V I S T

She froze, staring at the word, pulse tapping at the hollow of her throat. The cursor paused, held for a beat, then dropped to a new line.

N E X T

A chill slipped across her shoulders like a hand brushing the base of her neck. She pushed back from the desk slightly, her gaze flicking toward the keyboard on instinct.

It hadn't moved.

There were no ghost inputs, no sign of a lagging macro or corrupted field. The keys sat untouched, inert, as if they hadn't been part of the process at all. Slowly, carefully, she reached out and pressed the delete key, watching as the word dissolved letter by letter. As soon as it vanished, the screen went black.

She tapped a key.

Once.

Twice.

No response. The monitor stayed dark, unblinking.

Then, almost imperceptibly, a line of text began to fade in. It didn't appear as if it had been typed. There was no cursor, no input, but rather surfaced from beneath the glass, etched softly in dim grey as though the screen itself had remembered it:

You filed it. You carry it. You remember now.

Before she could take another breath, the line vanished.

The monitor blinked out completely, this time for good.

Overhead, the lights dimmed. They flickered once, not enough to go out, just enough to remind her that power was a fragile thing. Then they steadied, humming faintly back into place.

She checked the power outlet. Still plugged in. No scorch marks, no acrid scent of burning wires. Everything looked intact.

But nothing felt normal.

The journal still sat on the desk where she'd left it. Closed. Dry. Unmoved.

At least, it appeared undisturbed, until she noticed the spine.

Moisture had begun to gather along the leather binding. Not random condensation, but beads of salt water, emerging slowly and deliberately, collecting at the corners and trailing inward along the edge.

She reached out and touched it.

The water didn't smear across her fingers. It absorbed directly into the cover, drawn into the fibres of the page like it belonged there, as if the book itself was drinking.

She pulled her hand back instinctively.

And there, faint but undeniable, was the spiral, impressed into the flesh of her palm. No cut. No bruising. No pain.

Just presence.

A signature.

Her breath caught as she stood abruptly, chair scraping behind her, and crossed the room with sudden urgency. She yanked open the drawer where she had filed the journal, the photo, the report.

It was empty.

The folder was gone.

No book.

No documents.

No sign of the artefact.

Just a single sheet of paper resting at the base of the drawer.

Typed. Centred. Aligned with surgical precision.

Three lines:

> **You were chosen when you read the name.**
> **You kept the stone when you filed the page.**
> **The archive has always been yours.**

Her chest tightened. She backed away slowly, eyes flicking to the desk.

The spiral carved into the underside had changed.

It was darker now, not inked, not burned, but *deeper*, as if it had drawn something from her, or left something of itself behind in exchange.

She turned toward the door.

The hallway beyond was empty.

Still.

Silent.

But as she glanced at the glass panel beside the frame, her reflection stared back with a strange, unsettling delay, half a second behind her own movement. The lag was subtle but unmistakable.

Then it smiled.

Not her smile.

Something wider. Something older.

And a voice returned, soft, female, oddly familiar. Not an intruder's voice.

Her own.

"You catalogued it."

"Now you will be catalogued."

Back at her desk, the terminal screen flickered suddenly to life.

The catalogue software she had opened earlier had closed itself.

In its place, a single image appeared.

A new object. A new stone.

Not the one from Emil's photograph.

This one was different, its spiral cut at a sharper angle, the surrounding runes unfamiliar again, written in a pattern she hadn't seen before. At the bottom of the frame, two lines of text faded in:

The Witness Cycle: Object Four

The Erased Archivist

Then the screen blinked once more.

Black.

The light from the desk lamp flickered briefly, throwing a dim glow across the wood.

And underneath the desk, carved into the grain, the spiral pulsed faintly.

Slow. Steady.

Like a heartbeat.

The Archivist Before

National Library of Scotland, Edinburgh. Sublevel three.
Redacted Wing.

The rain came hard against the old city, pushing in sideways, smearing the high windows with a sound that wasn't quite natural. The kind of storm that didn't show on forecasts. The kind that arrived with purpose.

Dr. Malcolm Bryce was already underground when it began, beneath the main reading halls of the National Library, seated in one of three rooms with no official floor plan. He didn't look up when the lights flickered. That was nothing new. They always did that, especially when something *new* arrived.

The package had been waiting on his desk when he came in.

Oilcloth wrap. No postage stamp. No return address. Just his name typed on a thin white tag, the edges slightly curled with damp.

He should have logged it.

Should have reported it.

But he didn't.

He never did when things came this way.

Inside, as he expected, was a journal, water warped, edges flaking. There was a photograph tucked into the front flap, yellowing at the corners: a stone, roughly carved. A spiral at its centre. Around the edge, runes, sharp, fractured, distinct from anything in his museum archives.

And a note, handwritten on old letterhead:

From Lysefjord. Deep file reference: Witness – Strand, Emil. *File incomplete. Contents may contaminate live classification* *systems. Handle analogue only.*

Malcolm read it twice, then folded it back inside the cover.

He hadn't heard Emil's name in nearly two months.

The last correspondence had come as a flagged system alert, something buried in the field logs, not even meant for him. Just a general ping: *Subject inactive. Status: unclear. Record open.*

He hadn't been surprised.

Not after what he'd already seen.

The first spiral had come to him by mistake.

Fourteen years ago.

A mislabelled crate sent to the wrong collection. Supposedly pottery shards from a Viking wreck site off the Fair Isle. But tucked inside, wrapped in old newspaper and twine, was something else entirely.

A stone, black, oddly warm. Spiral pattern carved deep, but off centre, as if drawn while underwater.

It hadn't been catalogued. No museum claim. No field report. He tried asking around. Quietly. But people stopped answering his emails. One archivist retired suddenly. Another died within the month. Heart failure, they said.

So Malcolm kept the stone.

Filed nothing.

But he never forgot it.

It was gone within a year.

Not stolen. Not misplaced.

Gone.

He tore his flat apart. Filed an official theft claim. But deep down, he knew it hadn't been taken.

It had **left.**

He stopped sleeping right after that. Not entirely. But the sleep changed, became thin, layered with half dreams he couldn't shake. Songs he couldn't unhear.

And the mirrors in his flat started fogging even when he didn't shower.

Now here it was again.

Different stone. Different markings.

But the same **pull.**

Malcolm flipped through Emil's journal slowly. Some entries were in Norwegian. Others in English. The pages were stained with salt, not just warped, but *damp*. Still. As if the water had never left them.

One entry stood out. The pen was shaky, erratic, but readable:

I dropped the stone. I followed the instructions. The ship still watches. Maybe the offering was never for peace. Maybe it was just to mark us.

Malcolm tapped his pen against the desk.

That phrasing.

It mirrored a note he'd found in a different file, a sealed Redacted Order envelope from a disappeared archivist in Iceland.

He reached for his terminal to cross-reference the runes. The screen blinked once. Brief, almost like a hesitation. Then went completely dark. No flicker of warning, no error message, just sudden, full blackout. He pressed the power key instinctively, twice, then again with more force, but the machine stayed unresponsive.

The air in the room shifted. Not with a breeze, but with a weight, a subtle shift in pressure that felt less like wind and more like the floor had taken a long, shallow breath beneath his feet. He straightened slowly, his muscles tensing in response to something he couldn't name.

He turned back toward the journal.

There, on the last page, where the ink should have stopped, something new had appeared. It wasn't handwritten, and it hadn't been printed. The line had been gouged directly into the leather at the base of the page. Thin. Sharp. Deliberate.

You've read too far, Dr. Bryce.

His pulse jumped. He stepped back; eyes fixed on the words.

Then the journal snapped shut. Hard. No wind had moved it. No shift in the table. It closed like something had decided it was done being looked at.

He blinked once, involuntarily.

When he opened his eyes again, the light in the room had changed. Dimmer. Warmer. Wrong. The space looked the same, but the colour temperature had shifted like a dream sliding into another scene.

And his reflection in the security glass?

It wasn't mirroring him anymore.

It was still looking down at the desk.

Even though he was now facing the window.

The skin across his neck crawled.

That night, Malcolm packed everything. Emil's journal, the photo, the original spiral rubbings, and a hand-drawn map he'd compiled showing the location of every known disappearance along the Norwegian coast for the past fifty years. Each item went into a sealed envelope, one layer at a time, as if ritual might replace understanding.

And when he sealed the flap, it felt like he was closing a door he hadn't meant to open.

Not entirely.

Not yet.

He marked it:

REDACTED ORDER / Tier 4 - Witness Contagion Risk

To be filed by hand. Deliver to: Elias Verne. Section Head, Unclassified Coastal Artifacts.

Then he placed it in the dumbwaiter chute beneath Archive Sublevel 3. The one used when they wanted something **deep** filed. The one with no tracking. When he returned to his desk, the terminal had powered itself back on.

The screen displayed a single message:

THE STONE WAS NEVER THE DOOR.

IT WAS THE KEY.

AND YOU'VE UNLOCKED IT.

He looked down at his hands, expecting the same tired pallor, the same dry tension from too many sleepless nights. But something felt off.

A sharp itch had begun to spread across his left palm. Subtle at first, then more insistent, as though something beneath the surface was shifting, trying to break through. He pulled back the sleeve of his jumper, heart already braced against what he might find.

There it was.

Not a cut. Not a wound.

A bruise.

Dark and curling just beneath the skin, it spiralled in a slow arc toward the centre of his palm. Faint but deliberate. As though it had been pressed into the flesh from the inside.

Already forming.

Already his.

He crossed the room without thinking, hands numb, mind racing with associations he couldn't explain. At the far shelf, tucked behind a stack of old field notes and water-stained charts, was the binder he'd buried weeks ago. He'd filed it under anomalies. He hadn't meant to look at it again.

Now it called to him.

He flipped through the plastic sleeves until he found the page. A scan of an 1870s whaling log from Sørlandet. The ink was badly faded, but the symbols had been circled in red biro, his own mark from a night of obsessive cross-referencing. He hadn't known what they were then.

Now he did.

A sketch of a palm. Lines drawn. And at the centre: a spiral, etched into the flesh just like the one blooming in his hand now.

Next to it, a note in jagged handwriting. Not his.

"It appears first in the dreamers. Then in the listeners. Then in the remembered."

He closed the binder.

The lights above him hummed once. Flickered.

He didn't move.

The spiral on his palm pulsed beneath the skin, steady now, like a second heartbeat beginning to keep time with his own.

The next morning, the archive was silent.

Bryce's door was locked from the inside.

When they finally forced it open, they found no sign of struggle. No body. No journal.

Only an empty chair.

And on the desk, carved carefully into the wood:

Witness logged. Cycle resumed. Archivist erased.

Acknowledgements

Stories like this don't come from nowhere. They creep up slowly, built from the books you can't forget, the people who challenge you to go deeper, and the strange places your mind drifts when left alone for too long.

To those who encouraged this book even when it made no promises: thank you. For reading early pages, asking hard questions, and letting the spiral pull you in. You helped me believe in it and finish it.

To the scientists, divers, and researchers who spend real hours in dark, pressurised spaces beneath the sea: your courage and curiosity are unmatched. I borrowed just a little of your world to make this one feel real.

To the writers who shaped my understanding of what horror can be, strange, elegant, and profoundly human. Your fingerprints are in every line, whether you know it or not.

To the ARC team, thank you for stepping into these pages first. Your feedback, insight, and encouragement helped sharpen what needed clarity and deepen what needed silence. I'm grateful for every note and every moment you gave this strange little story.

And to the reader, for stepping into this story and letting it whisper. For letting it twist back on itself, and on you.

Some books end. This one spirals.

Thank you for following it down.

Authors Note

Some stories are told in straight lines.

This isn't one of them.

The Drowned Fjord began as a simple idea: a man studying the silence of the sea, and what happens when that silence begins to speak back. But it quickly became something else, a pattern that wouldn't hold still. The deeper I went, the more the story seemed to fold in on itself. Scenes echoed. Lines rewrote themselves. What began as a scientific investigation slid sideways into myth, memory, and recursion.

This is a horror story, but not just about monsters or myth. It's about how we interpret reality when it begins to drift. About the ways memory fails us or rewrites us. About the feeling that maybe we've done this before. Maybe we'll do it again.

Certain lines reappear in the book, sometimes word for word, sometimes not. This is deliberate. The spiral isn't just part of the story's imagery. It's in the structure. It's in Emil's voice. It's in the way the journal speaks before he knows what it's saying.

I hope the story leaves something with you. A sense of disquiet, maybe. Or the feeling that the spiral doesn't end when the book does.

After all, you've read it now.

You remember.

Aidan Blackwood